THE PETER LORRE
COMPANION

Anne Sharp

THE PETER LORRE COMPANION

A Bildungsroman

To order additional copies of this book, contact:
Xlibris Corporation
1-888-7-XLIBRIS
www.Xlibris.com
Orders@Xlibris.com

CONTENTS

1. BACKGROUND TO DANGER

I realize that the sex lives of Catholic high school girls may arouse a certain level of interest, and I promise I won't leave anything out in that respect. But I need to explain a few things first: like how I, of all damned things, ended up at Lads.

My mother was raised Methodist, which, as she explained to me, is Low Church. But she had always wanted something better for herself, so in her teens she converted to Episcopalianism, which is High Church. Besides, she sang and the Episcopalians had a better choir.

Now the difference between Low Church and High Church is that High Church serves communion, and this distinction turned out to be an epiphanical problem for my mother. She starting thinking one time about transubstantiation, the supernatural phenomenon by which the wine and wafer are transformed into the body and blood of Christ, which is then fed to people. She didn't like the idea of that, and went to her priest about it.

Wasn't it just a symbolic turning of the wine and wafer into Christ? she asked hopefully. The answer was no, you were supposed to believe that it really did turn into flesh and blood. But then you eat it! Isn't that cannibalism?

The priest said you just had to take it on faith. But my mother was no goddamn cannibal, and not only did she drop the Episcopalian church like a slimy rock, she married a Jew. Not a very intense Jew. He had never had a bar mitzvah, and wasn't observant. Both my parents were so alienated from their nominal religions, in fact, that when my sister Yvonne and I were born they took us to the First Unitarian-Universalist in downtown Detroit, where something perfunctory was done to us with water and a rose which did not impart any of the usual benefits associated with baptism such as eternal life or membership in a human community. But for years I didn't know this. Growing up among nothing but Christians, mostly Catholics, I had always assumed I was some sort of Christian too, and that I'd been supernaturally blessed as part of the collective routine, along with vaccinations and fluoride treatments. Imagine my eventual shock of discovery.

Now the public junior high that I started at when I was eleven was a hellish compound where 2000 hominids too old to be lovable and too immature to be trusted to drive yet were locked up for seven hours every day under the pretext of being educated. The real reason, according to Yvonne, who graduated the year I started there, was to make sure they weren't smoking or masturbating, and to maintain them in a secure area so they wouldn't destroy their parents' property while they were away at work.

Junior high hadn't bothered Yvonne any more than elementary school had. She acted in plays, played the oboe, ran for student council and had plenty of friends. But for me, my strongest memory of junior high is that roar every afternoon at three, when the final buzzer that released us went off, forcing me to cram myself into that stampede in the halls pushing out to the buses. I was always afraid I'd never make it out the doors untrampled.

The summer after I started junior high, my mother sat me down one morning and asked why I didn't have any friends anymore. Mom must have worried, since being an outcast was something she associated with my father.

ANNE SHARP

I couldn't explain. In elementary school, belonging had just been natural. You were part of a bunch of friends who lived nearby, you went to school with them, and all of you were constantly at each others' houses or going to movies or birthday parties together. But when sixth grade was over and it was time to go to junior high, all the friends who had seemed so close by turned out to be living in the district where the junior high-age kids had to go to Harding. I lived right over the border, in Sandburg territory.

When I tried getting together with my old friends after starting at Sandburg, it turned out to be so strenuous I just let it go after a couple of months. When I'd known these girls before, they were familiar to me. I'd known how to talk with them, play with them. But I didn't have the knack to deal with what they'd become in seventh grade, which was just like the big, fierce girls I had to face every day at Sandburg. You couldn't tell the nice ones from the mean ones. They looked the same, acted the same, until they suddenly turned on you. The atmosphere of tolerance for my natural weirdness that had eased me through the early years of enforced closeness with others that school consists of was nonexistent where I was now. I found myself a marked girl. People approached me only to taunt me, or more infuriating, to pity and adopt me. Whatever social skills I'd acquired over eleven uneasy years of life quickly eroded under these conditions. I slunk; I snapped. No, no friends at this point.

After my eighth-grade midyear report card came out, mom sat down with me again and wanted to know why my grades weren't better. I don't know why she asked *me*. I was thirteen and had the introspective powers of a potato. It puzzled me, too. I mean, I wasn't a "troubled teen," by her definition or mine. I never stole or set fire to things, I didn't have sex or take dope, I never skipped school or tried to run away from home. Suicide never seriously appealed to me. I even studied quite a bit. Every evening after dinner I took my books and shut myself up in my room. I sat at my white French provincial desk, with the little portable TV set Mom had bought for me on its corner, and did my homework. All through *Hollywood Squares, Hogan's Heroes, Dragnet,* and *The Merv Griffin Show,* I did

2326-SHAR

every bit of reading, wrote out every assignment that had been given to me. After that I'd be free to watch *Night Gallery*, if it were lucky enough to be *Night Gallery* night. And then if there was no reason to stay up after eleven—there were reasons; I promised I'd tell everything, and I keep my promises—I'd get into bed and read myself to sleep with one of my favorite books, Poe or *Dracula*, or *Great Tales of Terror and the Supernatural*. It was a regular and temperate life and there was no reason why it should have made me dumb.

And it wasn't like Sandburg was difficult. Between English, which consisted of boringly proving over and over again that you knew how to read and write your own language, and math, which since fifth grade had gotten so far beyond almost everybody that they'd never catch up, and cutting up stinking dead frogs in science lab, and copying out entries from the *World Book* for social studies, and watching cheap, risible movies about the dangers of L.S.D. in assembly, I wasn't getting exhausted from mental strain.

Yvonne once told me about an incident from her Sandburg days, when a friend of hers felt that his teacher wasn't bothering to evaluate his homework the way he was supposed to, but was just writing "A-" on everything. Yvonne's friend decided that next time he wrote a paper for this teacher he'd land-mine it with little asides like, "You're not really reading this, are you? You incompetent idiot," and so on. That paper came back with an "A-" on it.

Soon after I heard this story, I had to "write" an essay about Admiral Chester Nimitz for my eighth-grade history class's unit on World War II. Nothing much had ever happened to Nimitz apparently, as the *World Book* paragraph I was supposed to plagiarize for this assignment was so dull it was next to unrewritable. So I decided to liven it up by having Nimitz and his family celebrate V-J Day by taking off on their yacht into the Pacific, and never being heard from again. "Very interesting, never knew about this," my teacher wrote on the paper. I told my mother, which might have been one reason why she agreed to pay $500 a year for me to go to St. Ladislaus the next year, when we weren't even Catholic.

ANNE SHARP

There was also the day when my father went to my counselor at Sandburg to talk about how my mother was supposedly turning Yvonne and me against him. The counselor had called me in and asked me what I thought about this. I didn't know what to think. Mom, of course, hit the ceiling when I told her.

So when I came home just a few days later, hobbling after having been repeatedly kicked by a gang of hostile girls (which was not undeserved), and asked mom if she might consider sending me to Lads for ninth grade instead of making me stay on at Sandburg, if was as though I'd been a king and commanded it of her. Because within weeks I had a used green and gray wool skirt and a green polyester blazer with the Lads crest on it, and a pair of saddle shoes, and my name on the 1974 freshman class list. And mom had had a talk with Sr. Magda, the principal, before she signed the tuition check, about what was to be done about noncustodial parental interference attempts. There was understanding there, and so I had a whole new school.

I adored those saddle shoes. They were the wrong style, a bump-toed contemporary early 70s shape; I hadn't been able to find the trim, shark-nosed Oxford style I really craved, not at Thom McAn. But I wore those shoes every day (you can get away with that in Catholic school). And though it was fashionable among Lads girls to let their saddles get scuffy, I made every effort to preserve them, going over them carefully with white and black polish, buffing their matte finish and washing the laces by hand. Because *he* had worn them in *Arsenic and Old Lace*, and so they were sacred and beloved of me.

* * *

By the time I got my fresh start at Lads, my brain had mercifully ripened to the point where I could actually see some connection between my own behavior and the way I was consequently treated, and so get along with people again. In the whole time I attended Lads I was never kicked once. But it wasn't just me. Human beings in general improve tremendously between the ages of fourteen and seventeen. Adolescent girls especially tend to become more tolerant and affectionate towards one another as they get older. And so I had entered Lads—which took girls from ninth through twelfth grades—precisely at the golden age. As for boys, I'd never miss them. Since I'd broken up with my last boyfriend in second grade, I'd had no use for them or they for me.

So here I was, this former snarling dog used to bristling at the approach of anyone, malevolent or benign, coming at me down a school corridor—here I was walking unmolested through the halls of St. Ladislaus, passing for normal, nearly. Was it the saddle shoes and uniform that made them so indifferent to those same attributes that had made me a spat-upon Quasimodo at Sandburg, or had those attributes gone underground, successfully hidden themselves from public view? It astonished me now, the variety of strata of high school society that accepted me at Lads, that would actually pass notes to me in class, invite me to sit at their lunch tables: overachievers, "nice girls," burnouts. I could never bring myself to actually try to permanently attach myself to any particular group. I was too shy and feral still to think that anyone would take me on as an actual friend. But even this pathological alienation of mine didn't offend them. They let me float around the lunchroom, more or less welcome at whatever table clique I dropped in on each day. This state of affairs actually suited my latent voyeurism. I could stop and smile and listen, and they'd barely notice me; I'd hear the most amazing things. And it gave me an invulnerability. You're not at risk of being dropped if you never belonged in the first place.

Anyway, what would it mean to be popular at Lads? Did Lads even count as far as schools went? Not with those arcane Halloween creatures managing and supervising, and those outre dress regulations and behavior rules. It seemed to me that for a real high school experience, you needed the rich panoply of instructors and administrators a public school offers, middle-aged men and women wearing real clothes, who have some sexuality about them, or at least aren't pointedly denying their availability to everyone. Because sex is such a big part of your attachment to people at that age. You simply cannot have a crush on an ancient Polish nun or brother in a brown polyester habit. Unless . . . but that would be a step beyond even my adolescent appetites.

In past years the rules for uniforms at Lads had been very strict. Every day you had to wear the green blazer with the St. Ladislaus insignia and the regulation pleated plaid skirt with a white shirt, white socks, and black and white saddle shoes. But beginning in the administration of Sr. Benedette, coinciding with Vatican II, reforms were instituted. The blazer became optional except on formal occasions, and a matching vest was available as a warm day alternative. Sweaters and sweater vests could also be worn. By the time I arrived, under the aberrantly liberal tenure of Sr. Magda, students could wear pastel blouses and socks or tights coordinated with the colors in the skirt's tartan (green, gray, black and red). The saddle could be supplanted by any reasonably dressy gum-soled shoe. You could even wear Earth Shoes, very popular then among Ann Arbor whole wheat types, a sort of trapezoidal clown shoe with a recessed heel and elevated toe that supposedly held your foot in its most natural position, that of walking barefoot in loose earth or sand. Like the dead guy they all worshiped, trotting around the dunes sermonizing or recruiting fishermen on the shore. Maybe wearing them made them feel closer to *Him*.

Regarding clothes, thus far you could go but no further. Under no circumstances could you wear hard-soled shoes. (Too noisy? Or too hard on the linoleum?) Sneakers were out of the question outside of gym. And there was to be no rolling of skirts. On rare occasions a daring girl would flout this law and roll the rubber-ribbed top of her skirt over and over until the pleats hung at a more pleasing point on the thigh. Other girls might venture to try it, and this fashion fad would sizzle excitingly for a few days until the nuns cracked down and the thighs disappeared.

Back in the fifties, Lads girls had worn skirts that went all the way down to their ankles! I would have given anything for one of those skirts. That was the style for me. No amount of tinkering with the hem of my skirt (mom had only had to buy one; another advantage of parochial school) would make it fall at a more flattering angle on my knee. It wasn't just the length; the overall construction of the thing was a disaster for me all the way up. The pleats sprang out from the waistband, spread and strained to accomodate stomach and butt. The shirts bloused over the tight band of woolen cloth and rubber, filled with the rolls displaced by the corset effect of the waist. If I really hadn't cared how I looked I would have given in and traded in my ultrasnug size 10 skirt for a nice sloppy 12, but that was the female temper of the times, to go around like Cinderella's sisters, squeezing yourself into the form of a more desirable woman.

At public school you could deal with your puppy fat in comfort. You didn't have to nip in your waist or expose your legs to ridicule. You could enfold your flesh in your nicely broken-in jeans, with floppy tops you didn't have to tuck in. At Lads though the dess code ensured that your body was constantly exposed for what it was for shame, and this constricted drag of cinched waists and calf-embossing kneesocks needled me into a new form of self-consciousness, pointing out the difference between my chafed and red-welted self and everybody else, who seemed to move so easily in their uniforms. I grew to envy the really fat girls as much as the slender ones. The pain came in not being one or the other. The obese girls seemed so much better shaped than I did, rounded in once nice solid line, and they looked much more on balance vertically too. They even did better in gym than me.

Though the Lads outfit was cunningly planned so that when properly worn there was absolutely no window for adolescent sex lure, some of the girls looked pretty in uniform. And when you saw those same girls in civilian clothes, they were so beautiful you were shocked they went to the same school as you.

The common adolescent thing would be to imitate them, to try to be one of them. But I was too far into my own look by this time. My hair, for instance, which I arranged with ritual applications of rollers and Dippity-Doo into a sort of simulated 1935 perm—no one else was doing that. And makeup. By the time I got to Lads, I had pretty much perfected the maquillage that I would wear with gradual variations throughout high school. I was no conformist to teen magazine makeup advice columnists. I never saw the point of liquid flesh-colored foundation or powder, for instance. Why make your whole face look fake just to cover up a few skin blemishes? Still, it seemed antisocial to make people look at your acne bumps. So I would putty them over with beige-colored "cover stick" makeup. All those nights in the Night Gallery dug permanent bruiselike caves under my eyes, and I used the cover stick on these also, laying it on as thickly as I could get it to stay on every morning, with periodic touchups throughout the rest of the day.

Another consequence of my nocturnal habits, and the fact that I wasn't the kind of child that romped merrily in the sun, was that I had a sort of Poe maiden pallor that worried some people. So I simulated a healthy youthful bloom with pink or peach creme blush, high on the cheekbones. To bring my tired little eyes out of their caverns, I used Maybelline Thick Lash, two coats. Then, strictly against the advice of *Seventeen*'s beauty experts, I started using eyeliner; how I longed for the appealing melting eyes of a baby fawn! I used the liquid stuff. Very fashionable at the time, but utterly the wrong medium for a nearsighted girl. Brushwork is always more difficult to control than the stroke of a stylus, and the edge of an eyelid is not paper. I could never get down the technique of drawing the single uninterrupted fine line I wanted there on the little sill where my lower lashes sat. It always went on thick and jiggly, clumping among the lashes in hard little flakes it was almost impossible to pry off, and I'd have to work it with wet fingers and kleenex tips, dabbing in patches with the brush till the look approximated what I wanted.

The liner design was one I'd pioneered one afternoon after seeing an installment of the Taylor-Burton *Cleopatra* on the *4 O'Clock Movie*. (Every weekday Channel 7 gave you an hour and a half movie-and-commercial mix just before the local news, and any film that couldn't be edited down to sixty-five minutes got serialized over as many days as it took. I believe *Cleopatra* took three.) I was delighted when I found out later that Elizabeth Taylor had designed this eye makeup herself! But noted on subsequent viewings how I had missed some of the more expressive and flattering details of Taylor's creation. For one thing, my first attempts at replicating it had failed to circle the curved edge of the eye with the little pink baseball of tissue in it at right angles to the nose. This eventually became a deliberate omission because of accidents with the liner painfully flooding that part during experimental applications. So I would start off safely on the corner of the lid, and with my eye shut tight draw the brush along the edge of the lid till it fell off, then drag it further, again at right angles to the nose, another 3/4 inch, or longer if it was a dress occasion, to create the ancient Egyptian effect. The lower lid would then be drawn to match, again from a safe distance from the baseball to a point that intersected the Egyptian extension.

Then the pale blue iridescent creme eye shadow went solidly on the lid and all along the Egyptian line. If the blue covered the upper lid line, the liner came out again and the buried line was redrawn. The line that was drawn on the skin next to the eye tended to flake and spread as my eyes watered with insult at the reapplication of all these irritating substances; the poor things were only just getting over what was put on them yesterday, not to mention the smarting rubdown with baby oil that had been used to clean them the night before. So my morning's work wouldn't completely be wept away, the liner and the cover stick went along with me for repair duty round the clock.

The black liner was supposed to give me that appealing fawnish look. But those weak, sleep-famished eyes set so far back in my head meant that the cosmetic illusion of seductive doeness could only go so far, and after the makeup was completed and my gold aviator frame glasses went back on, the final effect was to make those eyes look flat, beady and sly. No wonder so many people thought I was on drugs.

One thing I did NOT do was pluck my eyebrows so thin that they looked like I'd been shaved and bruised and had stitches there. That style looked all right on Thirties film stars, but in real life, in color, in the Seventies, it was repulsive. There wasn't one girl at Lads who could carry it off, and at least three-fifths tried. But again that was the temper of the time, the Nostalgia Era. Bits of cultural ectoplasm were wafting in from a past we never knew, attaching themselves to our lives; we barely understood what was going on.

* * *

Right after my mother kicked my father out of the house, she started watching a film show on public television Friday nights hosted by Charles Champlin, then the movie critic for the Los Angeles *Times*. Each week they showed a classic foreign film and if you liked it, you got a chance to see it again when they reran it Sunday afternoon. So on the nights when all my friends in sixth grade were watching *The Brady Bunch*, I was sitting on the couch across from my mother and dog, watching something tremendous and adult and shattering: *Grand Illusion*, *The Cabinet of Dr. Caligari*, *The Seven Samurai*, *Ivan the Terrible*, *The Blue Angel*, *Knife in the Water*, and so on.

Not in a million years would my dad have let me watch movies like this. I had been an extremely phobic little girl. There was a talking clown doll, a Christmas present from an uncle, that made me run away and cry whenever I saw its face or heard its strangled artificial voice. Yvonne was fascinated by the uniform reaction she got from me just by taking it out of its box. Eventually the box was stored in the basement, whereupon I refused to go downstairs. It wasn't so easy to escape the *Romper Room* jack-in-the-box, though. During certain times of the morning and afternoon just the sight of a television set would parch my throat and rattle my vesicles. I couldn't even bear to hear that sinister, mechanical cranked-out rendition of "Pop Goes the Weasel" that heralded the Clown Eminence of Romper Room's imminent entrance, let alone remain in the room when that hideous staring red-mouthed monster sprang out of his tin casket. There was an even worse clown who came in my dreams to stare in my window. One night he came down on me in bed to smother me with a kiss, till I screamed and woke up.

My father got sick of having to get up and calm me down after such nightmares, and he retaliated by refusing to let me watch anything "scary" on TV, by which he meant "not for kids." So that meant *Romper Room* was fine, and so were Bozo and Milky the damn clowns, and so was all other programming that made me run mad with fright. Such as the ancient grotesque cartoons the UHF stations broadcast constantly throughout the day, with their gruff, sniggering villains and pathetic falsetto-voiced animal heroes, and those snarling, vindictive trees in *The Wizard of Oz* every Easter, snaring poor hysterical Judy Garland in their homicidal branches. Nothing in Charles Champlin's foreign film world, not even Caligari's sideshow or Lola Lola's house of erotic pain, could match such a cavalcade of psychotic horror, violence and misery.

Of course mom came to assess my father's censorship of my viewing with the same contempt she reserved for his other tries to rule her household. So the very Friday after she'd got rid of him, she let me and Yvonne, who were then ten and twelve respectively, stay up to watch a double feature of *Frankenstein* and *Dracula* on a special midnight edition of *Sir Graves Ghastly*.

Sir Graves was a child-oriented local television movie host on the order of Sergeant Sacto, Poopdeck Paul and Jerry Booth. Like Charles Champlin, he offered films that were decidedly not meant for nightmare-ridden little girls. Nevertheless, sitting up in the folded-out sofa bed in the living room next to my drowsing sister, I watched, not with fear but with a strange tingle of warmth, these ultimate forbidden films.

Frankenstein and Dracula. Karloff the cadaverous baby, longing to be dandled, raging at the shackles and teasings offered him instead. Lugosi the demon smiler, plying his voice like a gypsy violin: "Commm . . . hurrr." These lovely corpses stretched out their arms to me. Little girl, nothing to be frightened of. And there wasn't. I followed them into their dark worlds, came back wondering, moved, but perfectly unharmed. I longed to see them again.

So I pursued my tender Boris and racy Bela through many afternoons and middle-of-the-nights, all over the TV schedule—silly Sir Graves, with his embarrassing jokes and stunts, was not, thank God, the only panderer on my broadcast dial. And the more time I spent as a guest of these dead men, the more I craved their company. First I'd watch any movie with them in it. Then anything that was a horror film. Then almost anything that was a film, that glowed with the lure of a projector lamp rather than shimmering with the repellent sheen of video. I preferred films in black and white. That was the real color of movies. Color looked too fake-real-ugly. Besides, in the black-and-whites, the clothes and the settings and the men were much more beautiful.

So that's how I happened to be sitting on the couch that Friday night in spring, with the dog quietly snoring on the floor and mom knitting and smoking in her armchair, watching this film *M*.

You must remember this. There's a city made of grey stone where it's always night. All the people are afraid of a little man who slips around in shadows, emerging whenever he sees a stray child. First he flirts her into the bushes, offering candy, fruit and toys. Then he sticks her with the switchblade he uses to cut up oranges, and leaves her for her mother to cry over.

Every child knows this sort of thing goes on. Even before the child abuse boom of the 1980s, there were always cautionary tales of predators going around. Yvonne and I met our own big bad wolf when we were in fifth and second grade. There had been an M prowling our neighborhood in a black car, and he too had candy, although what he sprang on you wasn't a switchblade. At the time Mom had been working on her master's degree at Wayne State, and we girls were on half-days because of the teachers' strike, so we had to stay in the house alone for a couple of hours until she got home. One day Yvonne answered a phone call from a man who said he was Jerry Booth from *Jerry Booth's Fun House* on Channel 9. "Are your mom and dad home?" Yvonne hung up and called the number mom left for us. Mom came right home; she actually phoned Channel 9 and talked to Jerry Booth himself. No, he hadn't called. From then on, we had a babysitter in the afternoons.

So I was firmly on the side of those beefy, greasy old German men with the leather trench coats and cigars stuck in the bowls of their pipes, as they hunted down M the Knife, trapped him in a cage, and dragged him down to the basement to carve open his stomach and take out his latest Red Riding Hood. Get him! Get him!

They got him! Yeah! The little creep! He wriggled and shrieked and honked in fright. He crouched in the corner. He hid his face in his pudgy little hands. Then he opened his big round eyes, and turned to me, to me.

Oh, don't let them hurt me! he said.

He said it in German; they didn't translate it in the subtitles, but I heard it. Oh what big eyes he had.

He couldn't help it. Voices told him to do it. Everything would go black, and when he came to the children had become dead. How had it happened? And then the ghost of each child would follow him down the street.

Help! They're going to kill me!

There was nothing I could do. It had all happened years ago, and it was only a movie. Who knows if they were merciful to him? I went to bed in tears.

Again, they reran the Champlin program on Sunday afternoons, so if you liked what you saw on Friday enough to see it again, you had another chance. By this time, indulgent as ever of my privacy and not caring to put up with any more grade-Z Karloff films in her living room, mom had bought me my own little portable TV. I could watch what I needed to under optimum, intimate conditions.

What really floored me, what really almost scared me, was finding out he'd been there all along. In one form or another, he'd been there all my life. Not only through the moving image medium, but in the flesh, or rather the spirit. Like a dybbuk, he could take people over temporarily. Whenever the subject of murder, or perversion, or other weirdness came up, they would smile and speak in his cadences. But they "did" him so badly. What I wanted was my master's voice, the real thing.

There was something luring but painful to me about the timbre and cadence of that voice, that cello played with an over-rosined bow. The sound is unmistakable, in German or English. But in German, I don't know, maybe he wasn't perceived as having an accent, or what sounds he made were interpreted as normal, regional, traceable probably to nearby locales, Vienna via the Carpathians in his case. But the purling arabesques of his English pronunciation, especially as it hardened into the Mitteleuropaisch-Middle American intonations of his later California exile years, have tickled up so many sniggers. I myself accepted the occult loveliness of his voice with what I felt was the appropriate reverence. With horror, though, the truth came to me that I was constantly hearing people making fun of him. *Him*! On TV variety shows, on radio ads (especially around Halloween), on *Sir Graves Ghastly*, even on the playground, from the lips of my contemporaries, who had probably never even seen one of his films other than maybe *20,000 Leagues under the Sea*. I heard their mocking cruel ignorant mimicry and blushed and raged to myself.

It was also disturbing how someone who'd been dead so long could still be so much around.

Every Sunday morning I would get the TV book out of the *Free Press* and scan the movie guide, in consultation with the Halliwell's *Filmgoer's Companion* mom had given me for my eleventh birthday, to see if anything good would be on that week. A good film by now meant one thing. The fact that he had made so many meant that nearly every week he'd be on the schedule, sometimes two or three times, unfortunately all too often after midnight, which meant I would drift around most of the school week in a semi-hallucinatory state of sleep deprivation.

There was a sort of straight version of Sir Graves on every weekday afternoon, Bill Kennedy, a hilarious old prune of a former Hollywood contract player who hosted movies mainly from his old studio, Warner Bros. Which meant he'd show lots and lots of beguiling little programmers featuring that *other* studio-era Warners contract artist. What riches! It was great during summer vacation. During the school year, I had to get sick a lot.

It was better, really only possible to watch him alone now. My TV set had a little ear jack hookup, so in the middle of the night while mom and Yvonne slept behind the walls on either side of me, I could tuck the plastic nugget in deep and listen without revealing myself, spared that shame, at least. It was almost like the feeling for the basement doll, that unbearable searing sense of unease when he was near. Only this doll in his little box must be looked at, and when he laughed and murmured and screamed, I must listen.

I had no delusions of reference. I'd memorized the mortal dates in Halliwell's. I knew this was a ghost, really the ghost of a ghost, oblivious to everything and certainly to me. But this didn't make any difference. I felt what I felt.

It's astonishing how many people will ask who your favorite actor is. Don't they have any idea what a personal question that is? I would flush and stall, trying to come up with an acceptable reply. I must tell the truth or die. In the end I always died, though, because I tried to be frank, but would be pressured into betraying him. People would make a face and say, "Well, what you mean is you like his acting. You're not in LOVE with him."

I would nod and turn away. I saw mental hospitals in my future. He was so beautiful.

He was never the first thing on the screen. Stupid Hollywood must have known what they had in him. His face of a Buddha in repose, his iridescent purr, his beckoning expothalmic gaze, his body, that imperfect instrument articulated to numinous perfection by that master marionettist, himself. They deliberately teased you by holding off his entrance till the last possible bearable moment. My heart would go heavily, threaten to stop. Then he would materialize—and I could hear my capillaries crackle.

Every Saturday at eight I turned on my digital clock radio (digital clocks had supposedly just come out at this time, in the smarmy Seventies—ha! Karloff had had one forty years earlier, in *The Black Cat*) and listened to Jim Gallert's show *Jazz Yesterday* on WDET. The trumpet fanfare heralding Benny Goodman's "Stealin' Apples," the *Jazz Yesterday* theme song, was my catnip. Because it was the music of his time. When they played stuff from the late twenties, it was him in Berlin. Oh, yes, I knew what that meant. I was young, but I'd read Isherwood. The thirties and forties were him in Hollywood, his beautiful deft hand with a cigarette, in all those white linen suit-and-fern foreign intrigue thrillers. I saw his deliberate gests in Artie Shaw's clarinet, heard his low-register tones in Coleman Hawkin's

ANNE SHARP

sax and his soft, facetious faux-Asian falsetto in Django Reinhardt's sweet guitar curlicues.

Jim Gallert played jazz from the pre-postwar period, 1920 to 1945. The right time frame. Because after V-E day, it was pretty much over with him from what I could sadly see.

Look at *Mask of Dimitrios*, release date 1944. He was about forty then, button-cute, really quite slim for him (they'd probably fed him speed like mom said they'd done with Judy Garland, as part of Warners' fleeting, misguided effort to market him as a sort of miniature Charles Boyer during his post-Moto period.) As in *Maltese Falcon*, a pleasing love interest for croaking old Sydney Greenstreet.

Compare with *The Verdict*, 1946. The identical pairing, but what a nasty shock to see, and not just because the film itself sucks. I have never been able to watch more than a few minutes of it.

Something happened to his voice. I noticed it again and again, starting around 1945, worsening at the end of the decade and almost unbearable by the start of the 1950s. The lovely bizarre viol warped, became harsh and unpliable. Part of it was his gradual adaptation of our twangy American English consonants; that accentuated that scraping tonal quality. But there was also, especially in the post-*Verlorene* period, an awkward slurriness suggestive of the lingering effects of stroke. He sounded more and more like a mean impressionist's version of himself. And of course by then he'd been doing himself for too many years and knew it, and what an Escher's staircase that must have been for him.

And right around that 45 mark, no doubt for the same reason, his pliant, altricial features had begun to stiffen and freeze into the gargoyle mask he wore for the last decade of his life. This was particularly hard to take for me. I forced myself to watch some of the more important later films, *The Beast with Five Fingers*, *Silk Stockings*, the Roger Corman Poes. But it was always in pain and in mourning. Although he was he, always, and there were gems among the dross. That moment, for instance, in *Story of Mankind*, in which, as Nero, he reclines on his darkling balcony with a lyre, gazing with drowsy spent ecstasy upon Rome as it frizzles beneath him.

One night Jim Gallert played three versions of the Gershwin tune "Our Love Is Here to Stay," one after the other. I lay on my bed, marking time till 2 AM; Channel 2 would be running *The Face behind the Mask*, which I'd had to wait five years for.

The lyrics of that song cycled back and back, stinging the integuments of my heart as each vocalist took his or her turn with it. First the words were drawled and winked at, then rattled off by one who didn't care as much, and finally, satisfyingly wound up in a snug, artful embrace. The movies and the radio that we have today may fade away. He was alive when they wrote that, I thought bitterly. What did they know then about the ontological half-life of celluloid? or movies on TV? or the Nostalgia Era? or a fourteen-year-old girl trembling under this merciless thing that had crept over her when she was little, that she had hoped she would eventually grow out of, that she wasn't growing out of?

Movies fade away! Benny Goodman disappear! Microorganisms would devour me utterly before "Stealin' Apples" would cease to be heard, or he who'd died four years after I was born would cease to walk the earth in silver and ebony light.

2. CONFIDENTIAL AGENT

Because the middle of the night was when my life found real meaning, having to get to school by eight-forty-five meant getting up long before I was ready to. I could have slept in more, I suppose, but I really needed extra time to tempt myself out of the house in a gradual fashion. What I really liked was to wait till my mother was up, and then go lie in her bed when it was still warm and read the *Free Press*. After mom was out of the house I'd get up and have my soft boiled egg, toast and tea, and then dress and walk to the corner where my bus stopped. I hardly ever missed it by more than a couple of minutes. No great loss; I enjoyed being a morning pedestrian. The bus trip took nearly as long as walking did, as the bus had to dawdle all over, gleaning Lads girls from all sorts of little twisted corners of Prague, an irritating way to travel. Buses were a big thing at Lads. They even had them professionally blessed every September. Because so many girls had to be bused from so far away, from Westland, Redford, Plymouth, Dearborn, even Detroit. That's why school started half an hour later there than at normal school.

When you walked, you could skip the detours. Of course taking the bus ensured you would have ten minutes to go to your locker, work on your makeup and so on before the bell for home room, and on mornings when I walked I barely nicked being just on time. But I was never actually late, which was lucky, since tardiness, like smoking and skipping class, was much more harshly dealt with at Lads than at public school. You were supposed to behave yourself and be grateful they'd even let you in; you had to pay them to be admitted, after all, and they didn't have to take you.

It was a nice walk to Lads, nothing exerting about it. You went down the curve of my street, Palmer, then out onto Devon, the main road, for about a mile. The cars alongside you would be creeping towards the freeway at 25 miles an hour, wary of the patrol cars tucked into inconspicuous side streets that slavered to catch them speeding. ("Oh, the Prague fascist police force!" my mother would say adoringly.) You walked past dozens and dozens of houses, very much like ours because built by the same contractor, only most were bigger—even before we were dadless, we had the smallest household on the block. There were ranches like ours, and big colonials, all still so new they all looked the same, like babies. The first plantings of bushes and trees were still just striving past the twig stage, so even during the leafy parts of the year everything seemed bare. Bits of character were creeping in, though. Some of the more ambitious families had antique milk canisters and wagon wheels arranged on their porches, and there was even a little jockey over on the next block.

You passed chain link fences with excited dogs hurling themselves against them to get at you, and then my old elementary school and the swim club my family used to belong to, which my dad had always suspected was trying to discriminate against him. Then, as you drew nearer to Seven Mile Road, you emerged from my subdivision and had to pass some slightly older houses built on a plainer plan, tending to geranium planters and plastic ducks in front of the porch.

At the corner of Devon and Seven, there was the gas station on one corner and the Farmer Jack supermarket on the other. Across the street from Farmer Jack was the northeast corner of the Church Block, beginning with Marian Hospital, the cross-shaped brick mass where they switched babies and cut off the wrong arms.

The Church Block was a square block of land which the Catholic Church had presciently purchased before World War II, when the now-called city of Prague (pronounced PRAY-gg) was still Prague Township, parcels of gritty, mediocre farm land in an inauspicious interstice of Wayne County. After the Church seized this block and started developing it, they'd let parts of it go back to forest, which Michigan land is always ferociously eager to do. Now it was thick with conifers and bushes and meadow grass, and God knows what else. Into this little wooded mile the Church built the buildings necessary to lure the sort of people they wanted to Prague, and keep them there the way they wanted them.

So Marian was there on this nearest corner of the Church Block. Set in the woods beyond it, though I couldn't tell you where, was the nunnery, and other things related to nun life—there was a nursing home for old sisters, supposedly, and a graveyard. The sisters went into those woods at the end of the day to do their own business. Then at daybreak they came out again to work with people, at Marian, at St. Ladislaus (on Cloverdale Road, kitty-corner from Marian), and, at the north end of the Block facing Eight Mile Road, the Mother House Church and Fatima College. I imagined Fatima then as a luxuriant Arabic lady who led with her navel, like Amir Amir on *The Arab Voice of Detroit* (a sort of variety-talk show that took over Channel 62 for about a million hours every Saturday night.) It wasn't until junior year at Lads that I found out who Fatima really was.

Everything looked so old at Lads, and not just the nuns. Most of the schools in Prague were flat blond brick boxes with a flagpole at one end, each elementary, junior high and high school constructed from identical plans with Great Society money in the late sixties. But Lads had been built in 1950, the first year the city of Prague was officially incorporated. Lads had been made of red brick with the Gothic workmanlike care evident in an enterprise born of the early Baby Boom era, not really anticipating the massive child-generating exurb which would soon pop out of the surrounding sugar beet and pumpkin patches. Everything inside Lads looked like the handiwork of people who thought small and immediate and sort-of-cute. Cabinets were wood rather than Steelcase metal. Ceilings were low, as the architects had planned it all in womanly scale (women were smaller back then) and there was brick and wallboard where there would have been painted cinderblock in public schools. There was creamy blond varnished woodwork, raw red brick and philodendrons in pretty window box planters. Still, there were marks of austerity. In the bathrooms, the mirrors were small or nonexistent, and you washed your hands not in a faucet but in a huge, expressionistic-looking grey fountain you pushed on with your elbow.

Another thing about Lads: the cafeteria never smelled as bad as the one in junior high, that sour waft of janitorial cleansers and flour gravy. Perhaps that's because, after twenty-five years' experience as an all-girl school, Lads had more or less abandoned all pretext of serving "nutritious" food and offered only the sort of things girls between the ages of thirteen and eighteen could realistically be expected to eat in a lunchroom situation. Boys of course will eat anything you sling at them, but young girls have a more selective instinct, perhaps something to do with preserving the species. It made it so much more appetizing to have your meal offered to you without the grotesque pretense of decomposing salisbury steak and greasy cheap industrial vats of vegetable soup sickening in the steam trays next to the neat-to-the-eyes-and-fingers, individually wrapped packs that appealed to our sensibilities and sense of hygiene.

This was the pleasant place where I sat with my new near-friends, listening to them talk about cosmetics and hair and men and television shows I never watched, and young adult novels I would never dream of reading, and rock bands they liked that, unlike the ones I listened to, never wore makeup or chopped up baby dolls onstage or sang about psychosis or necrophilia. How tasty lunch was there. Wet steamed hotdogs and oatmealburgers on mushy white buns, and packs of chips, and Pepsi in big waxed cups, puny cartons of milk, the same halfpint portions that were supposed to be enough of us when we were six, which still seemed to suffice, and racks of what the lunchroom manager was resigned to acknowledge as the staple diet of teenage girls: Hostess snack cakes. Suzy-Qs were the clear favorite, with Ding Dongs and Hohos popular alternates. Sno-Balls had their following also, with their own protocol for consumption: the marshmallow frosting to be picked up with the fingers first in sections, then the cake consumed as a unit in bites, with a pause halfway to lick out the cream. Suzy-Qs, in contrast, were usually taken whole, though it was also correct to pull them in half. An occasional eccentric like me might choose a fruit pie, but these were usually the stalest for having sat longest on the rack.

No wonder my disposition sweetened, settling in among these sugared-up, saddle-shoed creatures. Their carefree blessedness was bound to rub off on me a little.

Whenever I am tempted to say anything against the Catholic Church (which is often in my line of work; can we ever forgive the Legion of Decency, and the Pope with his dreadful lists and encyclicals, for the leucotomization of the American cinema?) I breathe deep and slow—I'm a humanist, remember—and think of how Lads gentled me into its gray-and-green flock so unquestioningly, and gave me, at the age of fifteen, such an impossible, unasked-for and by then even unhoped-of thing, a friend.

It was Natalie Terabian, a girl from my home room. She was tall as me, maybe even taller, about five foot nine. And beautifully slender, not in a skinny way—she was just a narrowly-made person, with rich skin and hips and breasts that couldn't've existed on a woman who starved herself. The streamlined engineering of her body made her look in uniform strikingly unlike what any other child in the school would look like wearing the exact same clothes. The long, unbroken line between the underarm and the swell below waist level, the flat front from the under-breast to the thighs, the modest rise of her behind made her shirts tuck in neatly as a man's, her pleats drape gracefully without a gap. Her blazer hung as casually as a cardigan from her shoulders. Her saddles were perfect jitterbug-era oxfords with red soles (size seven, narrow.)

Her hair was straight but the type that will take a curl and hold it for days. She had big pink fishlips with sticky ivory-yellow teeth behind them. It was a mouth for eating sugar, and sucking on things.

It came as a gift from God, perhaps, that someone this beautiful should want to be with me. I can't imagine I had done anything to encourage her. We had Scripture class together—that was the rule, one religion course every semester, even for Unitarians—and had sat together at mass—no exemptions, even for deists; you just went and watched the others take the wafer. How did we get to know one another? I guess we must have sat together in class and passed notes. Most of the friends I ever had from school came from passing notes; in person I was gauche, but in writing I was able to reveal and hide myself in just the right proportions. However it came about, it happened that I woke up one Saturday after a late-night debauchery with four gorgeous old men in *The Comedy of Terrors*, and realized I was supposed to meet someone at the movies that afternoon. Natalie.

My mother, who hadn't been called on to drive me anywhere to see anyone in years, must have been pleased. I was supposed to meet Natalie at the Quo Vadis (which she called Quay Vadis, in that Natalie-talk way of hers). What did we see? I saw all the new films then. Every Saturday morning I would be sitting with the movie listings in the *Free Press*, trying to figure out something I hadn't seen yet, or hadn't seen more than twice, or wouldn't mind seeing more than that. These were the last great days of gracious suburban moviegoing;

talk about lost forever. There are people all over the country now writing grant proposals and holding capital campaigns to preserve all the old movie palaces from the twenties. But nobody writes grants for the places I went to as a child. They are shut down and resold, uglified, second-runned, cut up for more multiple multiplexes, chopped and chopped smaller until they fall down.

I remember my movie houses being big, certainly not compared to a Fox or Orpheum built in the 1920s, but nothing like these claustrophobic little tupperwares they shut you up in in the 90s. They had big screens; you needed space, an area many, many times your own size, in order to get the full effect of those monumental complicated faces they were showing then: bug-eyed goddesses like Diana Ross and Faye Dunaway, the manyfolded enigma of Dustin Hoffman, the weird optical illusion of Barbra Streisand, and that sad little crumpled Ryan O'Neill face. None of them were faces that would register at normal human proportions.

There was still the pretense then that films were occasions, real treats, and that the theaters that presented them should offer an atmospheric continuation of the magic they contained. Who will support a full restoration of the Mai Kai or Terrace or Quo Vadis back to their original 1960s-70s architectural integrity? The old studio-era urban cinema palaces were just shells of fakery after all, gilded and plaster-fixtured up to make you feel you were being entertained in a pagan temple, a European house of royalty, a grand opera house. But the lobbies of the theaters of my Prague childhood were meant to make you feel *you were in Hollywood.* The terrazzo staircases with the gold chrome banisters, the plate glass floor-to-ceiling windows, the fern-scattered rocky waterfalls, the purple plush walls and upholstery accented with white Roman statues, all gave an aura of glamor very tangible, because it didn't refer to fake Europeana or Orientalia, but to *your* world, your own very real starful, rich, vulgar, American L.A. You bought your ticket into it, bought your Coke, took your place in the scene, exactly as you would if you were in Hollywood itself, taking the Universal or Beverly Hills star house tours or poking around Forest Lawn.

So this was the setting for my social introduction to Natalie. She turned out to be a perfect movie partner. She was dressed to the nines in her suede jacket and fitted bellbottoms and frosted lipstick. She preferred Junior Mints to popcorn (less fuss, less noise, and far more stimulating.) And she shut up after the lights went down. (This was most crucial of all, to me. During a movie, just whisper "What did he say?" or "Isn't that—" and you'll learn what it is to be pounded into wiener schnitzel.)

After the movie let out, Natalie's mom came and got us, and we went to her house. I sat on Natalie's bed and she played me some records. They were nice, these records by young men who performed with just a guitar and a microphone and no boa constrictor. I stayed and listened till her mom started frying hamburgers with onions; the smell, and the gathering dusk outside, made me realize it was time to call for my ride home.

The Terabians had asked me to stay to supper. Back home, as I enjoyed my mother's savory macaroni, hamburger, canned tomato and Velveeta specialty that my sister called "German casserole," I felt so happy to be wanted by two households.

And then suddenly Natalie and I became best friends, the way teenagers become boyfriend and girlfriend, by mutual, instant urge and consent. We sat together at lunch every day. No more floating from table to table for me. Every Friday morning now, when we had our weekly all-school mass, I knew who to sit next to, or who to save a seat for. For the first time since I'd been stricken with shyness, I forgot myself and paid attention to a living person. People smiled at me now. Despite the continued necessity of hiding myself, I became familiar, almost warm, with other people: something had rubbed off on me. Natalie was enough to make both of us look outgoing.

I was dumb in her presence. Literally, I got stupid and couldn't think of anything funny or interesting to say, as well as just being unable to speak without forcing it. Part of it was that I seemed to have so little in common with her; what could I talk about? But then this dumbness was a habitual problem of mine. It was actually worse with people I liked. Yvonne once complained about how when she was driving me somewhere in the car, I would sit there for horribly long periods without saying anything. "Why do you do that?" she demanded. I was too embarrassed to reply.

But Natalie seemed happy to fill in the gaps I left open with her own voice. It's possible she knew that what went on in my mind was something she didn't particularly want to hear about, but I don't think her thoughts of me went that deep.

I'd come over, we'd sit on her bed and listen to her Cat Stevens records. *Buddha and the Chocolate Box, Teaser and the Fire Cat.* There was one song Cat did that I really liked, the one they had us sing at mass every week. There I'd be with a nose raw from a cold and my ears muffled from blowing my nose, hearing the muted sound of my own voice singing, "Borning has bro-ked, like the first bor-nig." Thinking that now, every time I sang it, I had someone to sing it with. And when all the girls stood at the end of mass and shook their neighbors' hands, saying "God be with you," there were pretty, slender hands near mine that would grab mine, with meaning.

*   *   *

Detroit has always scared the hell out of me. Some of the fear is realistic. I remember once I was dusting the bookshelves in my mother's house, and found a book from Wayne State University Press called *Race Riot.* I assumed it was about the 1967 riot, the one that happened when I was little. No, said mom, that was the one in '43, when *I* was little.

There were black girls at Lads; they wore raised-fist hair picks in their Afros and kept mostly to themselves. Wrapped in their Polish tartans, they were just ordinary Lads girls. But they were quite aware, I'm sure, how extraordinary their presence was in ultra-segregated Prague.

On the other hand, Detroit was *their* city. And any white suburbanite that ventured there must understand it was on the sufferance of persons whose tolerance of them had been rather severely tested. There was always the dread that some troubled individual would turn to you and say: For 400 years of injustice and oppression to my people . . . YOU . . . will pay.

Amid the sadness and anger of this beautiful, burned-out city, there were special places I've always loved. Like the Streets of Old Detroit exhibit in the basement of what Yvonne called the Detroit Hysterical Museum, a dark, cobblestoned recreation of what the city was like in the seventeenth, eighteenth, and nineteenth centuries. I also loved the Belle Isle Aquarium, a little dark hot cave with narrow, winding walls lined with greenish-yellow glowing illuminated tanks. Mostly the tanks were full of disappointingly ordinary local freshwater fish, but then occasionally there were some wonderful monsters, like the giant snapping turtle with bizarre starlike eyes, and the rippling electric eels that would show you, by brushing up against a bank of light bulbs rigged up at the back of their tank, what sort of voltage they had stored in their grey-black spines. I always hoped when I went there they'd have added some lampreys; I'd loved lampreys ever since I first had a craze for them in the third grade and included them in every story I wrote and art project I drew for school (to the delight of my Freudian-minded teachers). But they never had them there; I guess some animals are simply too revolting to be put on public display.

I used to have dreams about walking through those aquarium caves, afraid to look into the tanks because what was in them was too horrible. Then the glass would break, and I'd try to outrun the waves of angry marine beings at my back. Isn't this the ultimate critic's nightmare? The creatures on display getting their revenge? Even then I knew the score.

Detroit was then known as Murder City, the unsafest place you could possibly be in southeastern Michigan (aside from Monroe, under the lowering cooling towers of the Fermi plant). The safest place, of course, was Prague, guarded by its own Gestapo, glowing with goodness radiated by its Church Block. Between there and here was a string of suburbs loosely clustered along Hines Parkway. To the north were Livonia, Farmington, Plymouth, where people had definitively established a nicer sort of life. To the south were what Yvonne called

Wasteland and Garbage City and Stinkster, where people were not quite there yet, and might not ever want to be.

Natalie's neighborhood looked prettier to me than mine. It was older and the houses were all cute, even littler than my mom's. The brick looked better than our brick because it had had longer to season, and had been made with rich Fifties colors rather than washed-out late Sixties grays and tans and pinks. Her trees and bushes had had a decade more to grow, which made the streets look lusher; it also gave cover, making you feel less conspicuous as you walked down the little cracked sidewalks.

In my neighborhood you never saw people out on the streets except occasional children riding Big Wheels or playing football. People over sixteen never walked farther than the ends of their driveways. The only time you saw adults in their front yards at all was when they were mowing their lawns, washing their cars or using their snowblowers. Everyone had porches, but nobody used them except for showcasing their milk canisters.

At Natalie's the neighbors all sat out on their porches. And they went and sat on each others' porches, too. I was petrified with social unease the first night I stayed over at Natalie's. She took me across the street to meet one of her friends, and we sat for two hours with the girl and her parents, a father in an undershirt and a mother who was some kind of Balkan war bride, wild people to me. They laughed raucously, told dirty jokes with the kids sitting right there, with ME there. I remember the mother going to get a Pepsi for the father and him looking after and singing, "It must be jelly 'cause jam don't shake like that." Not in Prague it didn't.

Natalie's parents, though, never sat on the porch. I think they knew this was something to avoid if you wanted to give a better impression of yourself. Natalie's mother wasn't the porch type, anyway, and Natalie's father was seldom seen, in or outside. The only time I can ever recall seeing him, in fact, was a glimpse of this dark, calm man with a moustache in a corner armchair one afternoon, looking at his paper like "I've had enough today, this is the last thing I'm doing."

ANNE SHARP

Natalie's mother was the motive spirit of the house. She had two familiars, a gray toy poodle and a white one, tottery and high-strung, with brown weep-spots under the eyes. Stubbornly against early seventies fashion, being the sort of woman who knew what she liked and stuck with it, she wore an early sixties-style beehive, a peaked, elongated mound ringed with flattened curls that added about eight inches to her height, making her almost as tall as me. She wore glasses and pink lipstick and talked through her nose; in short, was very much like every caricature of such a woman you've ever seen in a drag show or underground cartoon. But just put Mrs. Terabian face to face with any counterculture snoid that tried to burlesque her; she'd flatten 'em.

She was very unlike those other Polish ladies of her generation who'd joined the Lads order and were teaching Natalie and me now; she'd gone the exact opposite route. Before she'd met Mr. Terabian, she had had a husband whom she'd divorced, which meant she couldn't go to church and take communion. That seemed sad and unfair to me. But I think Natalie told me that the priest could come to the house and give her communion there, which made me think a little better of the situation. I think I liked Mrs. Terabian. She was not unlike my own mother, a smart, unsheltered woman, tough through necessity.

Natalie invited me over nearly every weekend now, and we called each other at least once every night during the week. I must have somehow conveyed that I was glad to have her, because how else could she have spent all those hours on the phone talking, barely hearing a peep back, and have had the confidence to know the line hadn't gone dead?

What did Natalie think to herself, filling in all those big, fuzzy silences of mine? Did she ever get bored or impatient, wishing I'd hold up my end of the conversation? Or did she think I was a wonderful listener? I probably was. Whatever she said, I absorbed with all my being. Not that what she said was particularly important or even interesting to me. Natalie was not, by any measure, a bright girl. But she spoke unceasingly, and not very distinctly, through those sticky lips, so you listened carefully; it was easy to miss something. She never said anything mean about anyone, no gossip. She never talked about school subjects. No religion or politics. No stuff about movies or books. We went to movies a lot but never talked about them; as for books, I don't think she ever read one unless it was assigned to her in class, and then she must have approached it painstakingly, page by page. I'm just guessing; I can only assume she did her homework, since they never expelled her.

I barely recall anything she said to me in those early days. I only remember the sounds she made at me over the phone, with me curled in a corner of the kitchen floor, as far as the length of the phone cord would allow me to get from my mother and her blaring cultural television programs. I'd listen gratefully as those sweet, reassuring, nonsensical noises Natalie made absorbed all the nothingnesses I gave her.

*   *   *

One day my pretty friend gave me a pretty bag. It was soft royal purple felt with a golden drawstring, just deep enough for pens and things you wouldn't want to carry loose in your purse. She had one too. Where did she get them? From her uncle who ran a bar in Dearborn. A bar! All my relatives were teachers, on both sides. I was about twelve before I finally realized that everyone's parents didn't get the summer off. And the closest my adult relatives ever came to recreational alcoholic beverage use was the quart of vodka mom kept in the cupboard over the stove hood, which she and her friend Mrs. De Groot would take down sometimes when they were visiting together and wanted to have a screwdriver while they laughed and argued late into the night. They didn't use much vodka in those screwdrivers; I drank a lot more out of that bottle over the years than they did.

It was very hot stuff at fifteen to be sitting there at your little school desk next to your friend, with nuns and brothers just a few feet away from you, both of you fussing discreetly under their very eyes with your little regal whiskey bags.

Wouldn't there be some rule that we weren't allowed to have these bags in school? I really hadn't been around the Catholics long enough to know their convictions concerning such things. and I wondered about this after Natalie first gave it to me. But no, whiskey bags seemed to work the way cigar boxes for kindergarten supplies did. As long as what had been in them had been emptied out by authorized adults, they were officially cleared of their previous vice-oriented connotation and could be used for innocent purposes without remark.

But that beautiful drawstring that gathered and opened like a seductive private theater curtain was just made to be opened and closed on pungent and elegant things of adult diversion. When Natalie opened hers one day during lunch to show me a pack of menthol 100s cigarettes, also a score from her uncle's bar, I wasn't really surprised to see them there.

They really were the most gorgeous cigarettes. The smoke itself was not the best, the tobacco being coarse and hot-burning, but these elongated, fragile white paper pipettes with the little medieval-illumination leaves curling around their stems did have a way of making you feel, as the advertisements for this brand implied, like a very feminine woman. You felt it the minute you took one in your lips.

Smoking to me was an act of devotion. I took to it early and happily. Although everything I was smoking at that time had filter tips, I would ritualistically tap each new one end up on some surface three or four times before lighting it. Because they all did it *then*— Bette Davis, Humphrey Bogart, you'll see them all doing it, because the cigarettes they smoked were filterless, and you had to tap them to tamp down the loose tobacco that might otherwise get in your mouth. I honored that leaf-flecked time in memory. If anyone had ever asked me "Why do you keep doing that weird thing with your cigarettes?" I probably would have stopped, but they didn't ask me. Fellow drug-takers don't ask questions.

You hardly ever saw *him* lighting a cigarette. He usually already had one lit when the cameras rolled. With his little body so dependent on various drugs for its continued functioning, it may have been very important to him to have this one to clutch while working, something he wouldn't have to wait till between takes to administer to himself. Besides, the lighting of a cigarette, that suggestive gesture, was really for romantic leads; it wasn't part of the standard arsenal of a character man.

They were always shoving a lot of anti-smoking propaganda at us kids, trying to convince us that smoking wasn't really as "cool" as we thought it was. What fools they were, trying to take that tack. Of course cigarettes are cool. They make you cool. Their main pharmaceutical action is to calm you down and make you brave at the same time. It was his deliberate tranquility, along with the smoulder of that perpetual smoke in all those suspense and intrigue pictures, that provided the basis for his Americanized public persona. It was a funny thing to see this odd-looking little person, so self-possessed, with that ectoplasmic tendril rising from his childish fingers. When he was perfectly static, poised just so, you could feel his quick little mind behind the pose, and know something was coming. Like that moment in *All Through the Night*, where he calmly reaches for the ornamental box, in slow-motion nonchalance, before slamming it down on somebody's hand. Joel Cairo, Mr. Moto, all those unsavory exotics he played in the late thirties and early forties, were all variations on this quietly keyed-up stance.

It's a characteristic of small humans to be cute, to appeal to the protective instincts; it's a matter of survival. With small men, the tendency is to be funny, to get the joke started first before someone gets the idea of making something out of their subadult stature. When you are small, it's to your advantage to learn to be sly with the bigger ones. Through careful application, you will find methods of evasion and intimidation that will get you through.

The nuns may never have realized that our little purple bags were actually symbols of vice. Amazing things did slip by them. That freshman year, the cover of our yearbook was designed by some crafty senior editor to look like a pack of those very cigarettes Natalie had shared with me. Unmistakable: the leafy vines curling up along the lower edges and spine, with the little bare woman popping up among them, and the legend at the bottom: 400 Class A Women.

*   *   *

By the time Natalie came into my life, I was ready for her. Having a friend again, if nothing else, helped break the bleak routine of the Weekend Dad Dates that had started back in sixth grade. Part of my parents' divorce settlement had been that my father would have visitation rights. At first I thought that meant he had to see me on a timetable every week. But this never happened, and I gradually figured out that what the Friend of the Court was there to make him do was give my mother child support; the visits were optional. My mother was so contemptuous of the bits of money the Friend of the Court sent her she made a point of not using it for our everyday expenses, but putting it in a savings account for us to use when we went to college. What she actually wanted from dad was the money she'd earned after she went back to work, all those paychecks that she'd handed over to him that were supposed to have been for the family. Though she never actually expected to see any of it again, she would have liked to have known what he had done with all that money. It was dad's position, before and after she'd thrown him out of the house, that this was none of her business.

"I can't understand why we parted," he would say to me, years afterward. "We got along so well. And she was such a good cook."

I had had little to do socially with my father before he left the house, so when visitation rights started he had had to figure out a way to interact with us. What usually happened was that he would take us out to lunch (Yvonne would always order the most expensive thing on the menu, which made him really mad.) Then he would take us back to his apartment and go into his room and take a nap. That would leave us plenty of time to explore. We would look at his sinus medicine and merthiolate in the bathroom, and check the state of the vast vistas of canned tuna and kleenex boxes in his kitchen cupboards. We would sit on the chair and couch he had won from mom in court, and sometimes watch television if there was something really good on—Yvonne and I were finicky viewers. But mostly we would run around, up and down the big bare gaping stairwell surrounded by glass-curtain walls outside his apartment door, slipping outside the entrance to the building, where one sister would hold the automatically self-locking security door open while the other would make annoying noises over the intercom at dad's fellow tenants.

Whenever I would come over, my dad would have out on display this walnut shell with a birthday cake candle stuck in it that I'd given him years before, some little elementary school crafts project that was supposed to be lit and floated in water. I'd wince when I'd see it, this damn little shell tipping over in tiny patheticness on the Stiffel lamp table. I would usually try to ditch it somewhere, because this symbol of a lone man holding onto a demonstration of baby affection from a small distant female was just too gruesome to me. But dad always managed to dig it out wherever I buried it, and the dreaded walnut would be there to confront me the next time I came over.

They may sound bland, these dates with dad, but they were a little dangerous, always. Whenever he was scheduled to pick us up, we had to keep careful watch for him out the front window while my mom waited in the next room. There would be no doorbell ring to announce his coming, you see. He wasn't allowed to come as far as the porch, but must stay in the car. There was a reason for this. When the visits started, whenever my mom was out, he would take the opportunity to come in and poke around the house, which had been wrested away from him in the divorce settlement. Mom didn't like these intrusions, but there was no stopping him. That is, until we got the dog.

The real danger was in saying something. You could say anything about him when you got back, and were expected to—mom drew you out, with sarcastic commentaries on every bit of news you had to offer about him. Dad's technique was much subtler. He'd let you talk, not saying anything, until you slipped and put your foot in it—told him about some disagreement she was having with someone at work, for instance—and that would get you in real trouble, especially if you later admitted you told. You must never tell him anything about anything to do with her, because you never knew how he would use it. Or about yourself: your friends, your school life, where you went when school was out. Mom would always angrily remind me what happened the time I told him we were going on vacation to Toronto; we came back and found the house had been broken into, and half the papers in her strongbox were missing.

By the time I started my second year at Lads, I was the only child in my family that was speaking to both my mother and father. Yvonne had gone permanently over to mom's side. I'm not really sure what made me the hold-out. Maybe it was Scripture class; it made you think twice about violating any of the Ten Commandments.

So it was me that my parents had to make use of for mutual information gathering. I learned the discipline of the double spy. It took all my energy to be drilled in this routine, but I was perfect in it by the time I was fifteen. It was useful with people, not just my parents. Everybody liked me like this. They didn't know me even when they knew me: that was the essence of the technique.

The feminine tactics: sweetness of voice, smiles that vanish when the back is turned, furtive motions, sudden lashes of strategic fury. And always, when I could manage it, that cigarette.

*   *   *

Dad did take us places other than restaurants and his apartment. He took us to see *Let It Be* when it came out—that must have been Yvonne's idea, going to watch that sad, boring chronicle of the Beatles breaking up. It must have been a strain to come up with things to do with us as we got too old to take to the museums and aquariums. Yvonne the baby hippie and dad had definite clashes near the end about what things were good to do. Me, I went along with anything suggested. The only thing on my mind was movies, and my tastes were of course far too private to be shared with dad (though Yvonne knew, and was blessedly quiet about it). I wasn't going to suggest dad take me to see *Beyond the Door* or *Andy Warhol's Frankenstein*. He had no concept at all about this dark thing in me. He couldn't possibly have understood, I don't *think*.

Then again I remember one time he took us to the State Fair. I must have been about twelve, and Yvonne would have been fourteen. We had been to the fair a couple of times in previous years, though I'm not really sure why. It must have been Yvonne's idea, not mine, and certainly not my parents'. Mom and dad hated places like that; they never took us to amusement parks or the circus. When we were at the fair, we never did what other people did. We never ate any of the food, or played the games, or rode the rides. We just *looked* at things. We'd get dragged into the big fecal-smelling barns to look at the hairy, sullen farm animals, and to the pavilion where they kept the life-sized cow made of butter. I felt queasy about all these cows. I was still troubled by a field trip my fifth-grade class had taken to Lansing, when, during the bus trip there, one of my teachers had told us about something they were doing at the veterinary school there. They had taken a cow and installed a glass panel in its side, so you could see the workings of its living innards. This was so horrifying to me it obsessed me for my entire childhood. Just to tell a little kid about something like that seemed monstrous enough to me; I didn't put it past them to actually make me look at it sometime. That was why I hated the State Fair. I always expected they'd have that cow there. I wouldn't put it past them, them and their macabre butter effigies.

On this particular visit to the fair with dad and Yvonne, I came very close to that dreaded cow experience. My dad, not at any urging from Yvonne and me but on his own impulse, led us past our usual smelly barns to the very back of the fair, onto the midway. I don't know why he did this. He certainly had no intention of taking us on any of the midway rides. It could have been his own curiosity leading him there. He might not even have known why the midway beckoned, but had he known what was back there, would he have been capable of leading us into it? I don't know.

I barely even paid attention to the rides slinging screaming people around over our heads, but I stared as we approached this big metal spookhouse—one of those mobile home-type traveling carnivals things—because it was painted with monsters, including a huge likeness of the Lon Chaney Phantom of the Opera. This was pretty film-literate, I thought, for a state fair. There was, I think, a very inaccurate Frankenstein monster and so on also painted there. But what riveted me was a young woman rushing out of the entrance of the spookhouse, shrieking, I couldn't tell whether in fun or in real misery, but shrieking like something was coming to kill her. She wobbled in that space between the entrance and Lon Chaney, acting torn between dashing off into the mash of the fairgrounds and giving in to whatever was trying to will her back into that spookhouse entrance. We left her still howling and wrestling between terror and fascination as we passed on deeper into the midway, behind our dad.

There was another disconnected trailer, painted with lures to come in and see the horrors of drug abuse (I could feel Yvonne next to me stiffening in contempt), and then we took a turn and were in this enormous tin corridor, with the sun pushing down on us. I looked up at my father; he was smiling, his glasses tilted towards the lurid glare of the sun as he led us into this hot grim tube that went on for miles, as far as I could see, deserted except for us and the faces that stared down at us from that burning painted tin.

Bad blurry loudspeakers ground out shouted male voices, hurting my ears. I noticed Yvonne had her hands over hers. What they were shouting was horrible. Look and see what we're showing here! The two-headed baby! The woman who had a fish for a baby! Dead babies, lots of them, birth defects left unoperated on, defiant self-mutilators, green angry faces, corpse-gray stares over spraddled, disgusting bodies, daring you to look. It went on for ever and ever, and we had to walk through it, dad smiling and craning his neck at it, moving slow. I couldn't run ahead. I was terrified of getting lost in there, ending up inside one of those hellish metal boxes. We came to one box that had a woman in a bikini on display, fondling a snake; I felt so relieved to see an undeformed human body.

Then, to my gratitude, we were through the freaks, and into a line of trailers that screamed as loudly, were just as ugly, but not horrifically, just vulgarly, like a fun house with a German beer hall theme, with the loudspeakers grating out an obnoxious male chorus and animated figures in lederhosen swinging back and forth, gluttonizing out of enormous steins. And then even that was past, and Dad let us go straight home from there.

My sister angrily rushed into the house, and told mom about the offensive midway. "And the way they put down *women*! The Snake Woman, the Woman Who Had a Fish for a Baby!" I hid in my bed, with my radio under the covers, trying to block it out. More shouting made it worse.

Aside from these entertainment-based assignations with dad, we also got taken sometimes to what mom referred to as the Grand Relatives, my Jewish ones. I was never exactly sure how many there were of them. I had a grandmother who lived in mothballs at the Leland House downtown, and there were aunts and uncles who had children, my cousins, most of whom were grown up. My dad would mention them sometimes, so I knew some of their names. I thought it was good that I had a cousin somewhere named Melvin, as I was a fan of the Harvey Kurtzman *Mad Comics*. It felt it was an asset to me, this secret Jewish side, even if it wanted nothing to do with me.

*   *   *

So that was my personal life at fifteen. There was dad, and then there were the movies, those viewed publicly with Natalie and then those consumed in sensuous seclusion. You couldn't fit these three things together, dad, Natalie, and my private joy; there were separate chambers for each in my life, and none communicated with the others.

My mother understood my life. It was not dissimilar to hers. She had to dress in clothes she didn't care for and spend the day with people not of her choosing, only she got paid for it rather than having to pay; that was the privilege of adulthood. She saw nothing wrong with taking a day off in a responsible way once in a while, and extended me the privilege also. She would call Lads for me—I timed my requests that she do so carefully, not to abuse her courtesy—and say I was terribly sick, and then go to work, leaving me to myself, alone in the house. I would make a pan of brownies, eat a third of them, and in this heightened state sit down in the best seat in the house, my mother's plush chair, and wait for Bill Kennedy to show me *Passage to Marseille*, or *Think Fast, Mr. Moto*, or *Hotel Berlin*. Did mom ever look in the TV guide on Sunday morning and think, looks like I'll be calling Lads on Thursday? She must have understood the profound nature of what was going on, because even in arguments when I was being most hateful, provoking her to bring out her worst ammunition, she never threw this at me. She had no respect for sentiment, the feelings that made me keep seeing my dad, for instance. But passion she respected.

I could have collected him easily. With the nostalgia boom on, dedicated to worshiping the Twenties, Thirties, Forties and Fifties, they sold old movie stills at the drug store and classic radio tapes in the mail order record catalogs (ah, *Mystery in the Air!*). The home video era was still a few years off, so the idea of owning someone's entire film career in a set of little black boxes was still a science fiction fantasy. Most people didn't own films at all, unless it was their own home movies; only a few eccentrics collected 8 or 16mm prints and maintained the equipment needed to screen them. So the film experience itself was a treat, rare and cherished, and you fetishized movie artefacts in memory or anticipation of seeing the actual films. Prague had a movie-and-comic book store, and there were also similar movie buff shops in Farmington and Livonia, well within distances mom and Yvonne were willing to drive me to. Being careful with my allowance, I could have build a pornographic archive devoted to my secret amour.

But I didn't. I didn't even rip pictures out of books and magazines and put them on my wall in the usual adolescent way (though one gorgeous little head shot found its way out of my school library's copy of *Films in Review* into a small oval 1928 Jewelry locket I wore every day under my blouse.) I refused to be a crazed fan. I didn't fantasize him as part of my normal life, or crave illusionary glamor through imaginary association with him. Some people use love as an excuse for the most unforgivably bad behavior, but that's not my ethic. And delicacy and respect, I felt, were required with him. For he had been a great artist, and terribly misunderstood.

3. BLACK ANGEL

There was a look that was absolutely organic to Lads, that penetrated everything there that could possibly absorb style. It was in the way they made you draw in art class (at least if you wanted good grades), the look of the whitish-blond woodwork and furniture, the abstract wisp-and-slug-shaped designs on the covers of the books in Scripture class and the banners they hung by the altar at mass, even the brown polyester costumes the nuns wore. It was a kind of Vatican II Populuxe that seemed to be datable to the late 1950s. The 1930s were more my era, so Art Deco was my style. I hated every bit of this Ecclesiastical Moderne stuff, except for one piece of it, which happened to be the most revered and carefully tended object at Lads, so sacred we were only authorized to approach it on selected special occasions.

It was a carved stone Mary. Actually, this may have been cast in ferrocement, but the surfaces seemed smooth as flawless natural stone, chiseled in the curvy, elongated manner of a Brancusi, seven feet tall including the pedestal, with a face so smooth and featureless as to be almost nonexistent, an inverted shadow, as were the hands and robe and mantle, curving in the full beauty of uncomplication. Around the head was an iron halo set with white fairy lights.

This Mary was in one of those eldritch places in the woods behind Lads that only revealed themselves to outsiders if you made exactly the right approach. It was called the Grotto. It was a sort of miniature bandshell or artificial cave with a stone or concrete altar in the shadow of its archway and two curving rows of benches made of the same stuff set in front of it. The Grotto seemed small, crowded on all sides by unmowed meadow grass and trees, but on the day they brought us there to worship Her, our entire class fit perfectly on those few little benches. Maybe they multiplied like the loaves and fishes.

This first time I saw Her was on a May morning. They had brought us there not for an ordinary Mass, but some other ritual that none of them seemed too familiar with. They gave us all mimeographed programs to follow, and I noticed the other girls were studying them as carefully as I was.

Brother Tom, one of our religion teachers, led the service. What it was, it turned out, was a special rite for Her, a rite of spring. There is a time in southeastern Michigan technically referred to as spring, which is usually just a sloppy, extended species of winter, but this day was actually a genuine Easter basket spring day, with deep green grasses and little yellow buds, and a breeze making tiny movements through our hair and the mimeoed pages in our hands. Warmed in the mild sunshine, we began the main part of the service, which was called a Litany, a chant in Her honor, led by Brother Tom.

He sang an eerie line of melody in his mellow tenor, a sigh that rose and fell, which we then repeated in our high-pitched female blur, following the words in our programs. Then he would sing the same melody again, only with different words, a new line in honor of Her, singling out some new praiseworthy thing to tell Her about some virtue She possessed, some wonderful, merciful thing She did for us that made us love Her. The lovely call and response went on and on: it seemed there was no end of praising Her. That soft weird chant felt so pure coming out of our throats that we couldn't have tired of it if we had gone on all day. We might have gone on forever, sitting in our stone circle, calling out to Her as the angels are supposed to do in Heaven, but the words ran out on the printed sheets and Brother Tom stopped us.

*   *   *

The Church Block must have been configured to shift shape, contract and gain mass as necessary to keep hidden all that was contained there, especially in those woods beyond the Grotto. What did they do in there, those nuns? My friend Ruthie swore she saw two of the younger ones climbing out of the grass once, pulling down their skirts. Woo hoo! though it was hard to imagine.

A friend of my sister's who used to live in the subdivision across from the Church Block told me a story once about her rotten teenage adventures, which her parents had tried to curb by grounding her. In order to sneak out at night without them knowing it she would steal the metal box that the milkman left the milk in off the front porch, put it under her bedroom window and use it as a stepping stone when she wanted to climb out. Her parents would wonder why the milk box kept turning up under her window, and finally decided she must put it there for her friends to stand on when they came by to visit her while she was grounded.

This friend of my sister's had wanted to go to a party one evening that was going on at a friend's house about half a mile away, east of Devon Road, and she'd decided to cut across the Church Block to get there instead of taking the long way around. She went in by the Lads entrance, went past the school building and tennis courts and into the woods.

She felt lost. There was no path and it was too dark to see any landmark that might tell her she was still going in the right direction. Then she came on a clearing, and suddenly found herself in a grave-yard. Something moved; she screamed. It was a deer, but a big deer with sharp hooves coming at you in the dark is no joke. She ran and smashed her way to the other side of the Church Block, and then limped all the way to the party, where they gave her a very badly needed drink.

*   *   *

It was the summer after my freshman year at Lads when my father got married. His bride sent me an invitation. Although by this time my dad probably didn't expect my sister to show up for this event, he expected me, and was very hurt and puzzled when I didn't come. The fact that I hadn't learned to drive yet, and could hardly have asked mom or Yvonne to take me there in our car, didn't occur to him. I suppose I could have gotten a cab.

This was the official end of my family. My mother hardly got out of bed the week it happened, and Yvonne mostly stayed away with her friends. The house hadn't been dusted since the last time I'd done it, which had probably been sometime in April. By the time the actual marriage had happened, I could barely talk or even move, and everything made me cry. I asked my mother if I could see a psychiatrist. She was outraged, telling me she could see through my plan to show my father what he wanted to see, that we'd fall apart without him. But Mrs. De Groot had a talk with her and urged her to send me to Dr. Sherameta, a child and family therapist who she'd met at some sort of values clarifications workshop and thought was wonderful.

The first time I met with Dr. Sherameta, she asked me whether I was a virgin and how often I played with myself. The second time she listened to me talk about my family and sob. The third time she listened a little more, then told me these things happen to a lot of people, and I ought to start doing activities that would get me out more, like skiing. The fourth time I said nothing. The fifth and sixth time I told her how much better I felt and how well things were working out, and she smiled. Then I crawled back into my dusty house and there was no seventh time.

*   *   *

The film *M* was the product of a deliquescent marriage. One of the last things the half-Jewish filmmaker Fritz Lang did with his increasingly Nazified wife, Thea von Harbou, was write the scenario for it. There's some discussion in the literature about which real-life criminal or criminals inspired them to invent the little child-murderer in *M*, but I think the Victorian Englishman Jack the Ripper was an obvious forefather, with his similar modus operandi of alfresco urban predation and swift slashing attack. The Langs themselves admitted to creating the film to capitalize on the publicity stirred by a plague of serial killings that had recently fascinated Weimar Germany (just as Alfred Hitchcock, Tobe Hooper, Jonathan Demme and other filmmakers would later cash in nicely on the multiple-murderer boom in America). Some of the murderers in the news when Lang and Harbou created *M* are even mentioned in the film, such as Fritz Haarman, the bloodthirsty pederast who's often cited as the "real" M.

Also mentioned by some sources as a possible M candidate is Peter Kürten, a rape-murderer known as the Vampire of Dusseldorf, who became the subject of a groundbreaking 1932 forensic psychology treatise, *The Sadist*. Whether or not the Langs had Kürten particularly in mind, his trial and sentencing took place more or less concurrently with the making of *M* the international media event, and before he was executed he may have taken satisfaction in his implied association with the scandalous success of this new film and its twenty-six-year-old featured player, with his haunting tadpole face and chalkmarked overcoat.

Like others of his predatory ilk, Kürten was the very opposite of the pathetic little puppet of fate dreamed up by Mr. and Mrs. Lang. A slick, shrewd operator who enhanced his good looks with touches of makeup before he went on the prowl, he never heard voices or feared ghosts after he killed; he bragged of masturbating at his victims' graves. Near the moment of his execution, he asked lasciviously if his severed head would be able to hear the blood gushing from the stump of his neck, implying that this would trigger his ultimate orgasm.

As for that other Peter, he never did come to comfortable terms with his status as the world cinema's first great serial killer. There was one particular repercussion of that strange fame, however, that he might have appreciated, had he known about it. It seems that one evening during the late 1970s, the man known in the Los Angeles papers as the Hillside Strangler and his henchman were shaking down a young woman they'd chosen as their latest rape-torture-murder victim. But when they went through her wallet, the name on her driver's license and a picture of her as a child sitting on her father's

ANNE SHARP

lap made them decide to let her go. Cathy Lorre later appeared as a witness for the prosecution at their trial, helping to nail the bastards. We, too, should keep a closer watch on our children.

* * *

I had no reverence for teachers then, but I was used to confining myself to snickering behind their backs. You tended not to let teachers in public school know directly how you felt about them. They were tough and overeducated, and smacked you down if you got snippy. I was taken aback at the vulnerability of some of the older nuns they sent in to teach us at Lads, and at some of the liberties the girls took with them. There were just a couple of incidents that I remember. Nevertheless, to me it took an astonishing nerve to do this. Iif you snotted off to a teacher in public school, you just had the principal to worry about, but these were the brides of Christ.

The girls didn't pick on all the nuns. Just the very elderly ones. Public school put its teachers out to pasture at least fifteen years before the Pope did, from what I could see. Some of these crookbacked little ladies looked to be in their seventies if not their eighties, and that's no time of life to be dealing with adolescent harpies of even a relative tameness, like we were.

One of the nuns who came in for the worst of it was Sr. Anya, a tiny, long-beaked woman with insecure dentures, whose faded, folded skin was like delicate old latex. She taught us grammar, a compulsory ordeal none of us could forgive her for. They'd questioned our spelling, we were used to that, but no one had ever challenged our command of our own language to this profoundly insulting an extent, and it was especially hard to take from this whistling little old Pole. We could never follow the insane rules she set for us, at least to her satisfaction. I was sick of her constant markings-up of my effortfully diagramed sentences, underlined and formatted in the styles and ink colors she'd demanded we use. She persecuted every aspect of our scholarship, down to the very circles and stars and flowers over our

"I"s, which she made us turn into unexpressive, boring dots. That act of joy-killing censorship was the last straw for me.

So I laughed the morning one of the more distasteful girls put a note on Sr. Anya's lectern that said, "You sexy thing." "I believe in miracles!" the girl sniggered as she took her place among us for the ensuing show.

Sr. Anya, who prized a sort of reserved Atticus Finchlike demeanor when confronted with defiance, wiped the figurative spit from her face with her hanky and demanded to know who . . . *who*. We stonewalled her. No one said a word. Diagram *that*, sister.

Facing another wall of young stone faces was Sr. Bozena, the target of a subtler campaign of faint whistles, barely there, but pitched to abrade the most sensitive decibels still audible to a woman her age. It was Professor Unrat time. Little Sr. Bozena, a dark, beetling version of Sr. Anya, made us stand in a line across the room and not speak or move till we would presumably break under the strain and confess who had done . . . *this*. But we were young and for the most part well-rested, with plenty of calcium in our nice straight spines. We stood without a peep till the bell rang, then sprang away without a look at her. Gonna go home and tell your husband on us, Bozo?

*　*　*

When Mrs. Terabian decided to send Natalie to modeling school, it probably wasn't with any intention of having her model professionally; she just felt she needed polishing. Any woman who took as much trouble with her own hair as Mrs. Terabian did would definitely want to polish her daughter. Besides, just looking at me, she could see the consequences of allowing your child to pick up her grooming hints from the *4 O'Clock Movie*.

The people at the modeling school loved Natalie. They praised her statuesque height, her eyes and cheekbones, her small hands and feet. They gave her a diet that brought her down from a size 8 to a 6. That's great, I said, speaking as a 10.

"I dint know," giggled Natalie. "They say they really want to get me down to a 4."

One Saturday morning I came over to find Natalie eating cereal and milk, definitely not on her modeling school's menu planner. She laughed and told me she wasn't allowed to diet anymore; she'd fainted the other day. Why!

"Well, I hadn't eaten anything since day before."

I asked what it was like to faint.

"I dint know. . . . I was just standing here by the table, and then I was on the floor."

So Natalie's breasts weren't to be starved away after all; they hung as robustly as ever. Still, what the modeling people couldn't do to her body, they could make up for with cosmetics. Mrs. Terabian bought Natalie a vanity mirror with light bulbs all around it, which could be switched to two modes of brightness, evening and daytime. I spent hours watching Natalie and that mirror, picking up tips such as how to get that infuriating liquid eyeliner to go on straight (you HAD to keep your eyes open) and the right way to pluck your eyebrows (from underneath, never from the top). So modeling school was valuable for both of us.

* * *

It was in the spring of tenth grade that Natalie had her first official boyfriend. He was not terribly impressive. He lived down the street from her, was husky and double-chinned and quiet, and his biggest turn-on was bondoing his Stingray. But he was a real boyfriend who took her to the park and kissed her.

I knew what went on with him and her. Every detail of their dates was reported to me during those long, one-sided phone conversations Natalie had with me, and so I knew it was no tragedy when Natalie lost interest and segued into a new romantic situation. I never met this other guy, but he was apparently much more satisfactory than the Stingray guy. He had more flair, bringing her flowers and taking her to dinner; for another thing, he did more. I mean did more.

That was such a carnal time, when I was growing up. You were constantly being told that sex was natural and fun, and that the only real perverts were the ones who didn't have it at all. But most of the sexuality I saw represented in films and books and songs and Yvonne's underground comic books and heard bragged about at school seemed as unconnected to my own desires as the behavior of mating dogs. The lovemaking that I intended to engage in wasn't really of the body; sheer physical ecstasy I could take care of myself. I did not yearn for penetration as an end in itself. I was no universal female connection seeking a plug. Of course, I wasn't exactly in demand among boys my age. Not being blonde and thin with enormous breasts and a lip-glossed pout, I was a living affront to human reproductive biology in the *Hustler*-fed frame of reference of most of the males I ran into. But I could see for myself that I was a rather fine specimen. Current mass media fashions in female body styling might be against me, but the European galleries of the DIA were full of paintings of my body, my skin tones; Victorian engravings were full of the outlines of my full-cheeked face; my very thighs were flashed by Dietrich astride her barrel on the stage of the Blue Angel. My hips are wide, my breasts are firm. Such women, they say. . . .

As I matured, let my hair grow into more natural lengths and lost more and more puppy fat as nicotine sped my metabolism, I thought I was turning out rather well. I'd find that perfect eyeliner someday. I was Unitarian after all, and believed in the ultimate perfectibility of humankind.

What Dorothy Parker said about girls and glasses was true in my case, and a blessing. To be felt up and lied to by a boy my own age wasn't something I needed or craved. What I wanted was a *man*, and not the ordinary Prague man. He would be beautiful, but in a way only I could see. Because he would be *weird*, this man, even weirder than me. That was how I would recognize him. And I'd have to come when he beckoned to me. That was what I was made for.

For an untouched girl who spent most of her time with Catholics, I had very advanced views on the subject of birth control. I had every intention of using it someday. Also, I had seen that famous, horrible old black-and-white police photo of a bare, doubled-up dead woman, collapsed in a pond of her own blood, and understood its grave message. I would hear people talk about stopping abortion by making it illegal again, and wonder how they could be so stupid. I understood even then that desire leads you to places you sometimes need a hand to get out of.

So I had very decided convictions on this topic that day when I was standing by Natalie's locker, waiting for her to get her things organized so we could go to lunch, and noticed a little newsprint religious comic book she had taken out of her purse. I don't think she got it at Lads because I hadn't seen such a thing passed around there before; she must have gotten it at catechism. It was about what abortion was and it illustrated all the ways it was done, with a little cartoon baby with curlicued forehead and single front tooth standing in for the foetus (which I knew looks more like a cocktail shrimp than a human baby at the time of most abortions). The baby was reacting with the same expression of wide-eyed squalling protest to being sliced up like a potato with a scalpel, liquefied by vacuum expression, scalded with saline solution, and so on. I thought this was a pretty tasteless thing to give to kids, not to mention misleading. For one thing, this cartoon baby was floating in air; you never got the impression that it was contained in or connected to the body of an actual human being.

This comic book must have been part of a new campaign launched at Catholic youth because not long after I saw Natalie's copy of it we had an all-school assembly for the purpose of showing us what, according to the Church's point of view, abortion is all about. Only this was a slide show, using what they told us were real pictures taken at an actual hospital.

I remember the opening slides, set in a dirty-looking clinic, photographed in the squalid, darkish lighting one often sees in pornographic pictures. I remember the old nun who narrated the slide show saying, "There's a very honorable tradition among the blacks where the women will have their illegitimate babies." All the black girls in the auditorium were probably very flattered by that. Now, was this going to be a dilation and curettage, D and E, or a saline? Too bad, I wasn't going to find out.

I was surprised to see another girl had gotten out to the hallway before me; it was Bonnie, a thin, delicate, nice girl I'd always rather liked. "I couldn't stand it!" I said indignantly.

"I couldn't either," Bonnie replied queasily.

I guess the nuns had thought we'd both run out to throw up, which is why they didn't come after us and make us go back in. For the first time since I'd started at Lads, I asked myself: who are these people, these people I'm with? Who are the people running this school, and what do they think of me? They treated us like such delicate maidens, on the one hand. The roughest book they ever gave us to read was *The Red Pony*; the show they'd chosen for us to do as our school musical last year was *Little Mary Sunshine*; at our last school assembly, they'd shown us *Rose Marie* (with *Jeanette MacDonald* and *Nelson Eddy*! Who in that school besides Sr. Anya and Sr. Bozena and me could have possibly appreciated such a quaint antiquarian spectacle?) Now they were shoving this spreadeagled gynecological horror show in our faces, and why?

I felt so insulted. Of course I had every intention of having sex one day. But I planned to use a diaphragm, or maybe have a baby by each great love of my life, like Vanessa Redgrave in *Isadora*. I was not *intending* to ever do what they were talking about in there! And what about those girls still in that auditorium, those holy virgins who were supposed to be saving themselves for their wedding nights! Why should they be subjected to this, if the nuns had done their duty and instilled the proper chasteness in them?

To me they were saying: We are playing a game, pretending that you're still children, that you're all good girls. But we know what you really are. We know what you want to do. And then, when you're done with *that*, you'll want to do THIS!

My unviolated body, my abstemious behavior meant nothing to these people. To them, I was already a busted cherry, the little shrimp of my womb even now palpably mushed at the bottom of a suction bottle. As far as innocence went, I didn't deserve the respect that went with the benefit of the doubt. I just had to be made sick, because I made them sick.

* * *

One Saturday afternoon Natalie's modeling school sponsored a show at Falzon's, a restaurant on Eight Mile not far from my house. Natalie invited me to come see it, since I was so close. I didn't even need mom to drive me there; I just bicycled over.

Falzon's was one of those old-fashioned steak-and-scotch road-houses popular with Prague businessmen then. My mother claimed it was really a Mafia hangout, and that she'd heard Liza Minnelli had come there in secret one night to entertain at a private party of local dons. It really was an appropriate gangster hangout, all dark and wrought with black iron and blood-colored leather. I sat by the door with a ginger ale, for which they'd charged me a dollar, the rack-eteers.

It turned out to be a lingerie show. A cheery, pretty lady from the modeling school came up on the little platform where Liza Minnelli herself might have performed, and from a little pack of index cards read off the particulars about what each girl was modeling and how much it was (the lingerie, not the girl). Each girl came out from behind the platform and stopped by the tables in turn, making a pirouette so the garment she modeled could be examined from all sides, then did a final walk back along the bar as the next girl emerged.

Next to the bar, across from where I was, stood another lady from the modeling school. If not Mrs. Terabian's sister, she was defi-nitely of her school, with her crown of rose-gold ringlets pulled tautly back from a shiny forehead, her pink-rouged lips pursed angry over a thrusting triple chin. She was ready to kick over and stomp the teeth out of any man who dared even twiddle the fabric on one of her girls. The men knew it, too. Already at the age and girth that threatened heart attack, they moved uneasily in their mahogany captain's chairs as the daughter-aged nymphs slithered against their suited shoulders in passing.

"And now here's Natalie, all ready for a day at the beach—" From behind the blood-velvet drapes Natalie pranced in in a lavender string bikini that no sane girl would ever have worn on a public beach, let alone in the water. Natalie's eyes glinted, her sleek hair glowed, her moist teeth caught the light of the ruby-glass lanterns in a frank smile of delight. She didn't bounce or wiggle; she didn't need to. Her innocent lithe young body, her honey skin looked more appetizing than any airbrushed, silicone-packed porno image ever could. The men were dying as she brushed past them. She met every eye that looked at her with a steady gaze. By the end of the show, she was the only one smiling.

4. The Man Who Knew Too Much

"You don't need to sight read," Yvonne told me, long distance from college. "Billie Holiday couldn't and she wrote songs!" A few days later through the mail came a little brown paper-wrapped parcel: a tape. It was the soundtrack of the Ken Russell film version of *The Boy Friend*, a treasure from the collection of one of her theater professors. Yvonne must have loved me, to beg the disc from him and risk the eviscerated death that would have resulted from her having scratched it, for the sake of recording it for me.

I had seen the Russell *Boy Friend* once on television, and absolutely hadn't gotten it. Hard-core Russell isn't something you get hooked on just like that; usually there's a gateway drug involved, like *Women in Love* or *Tommy* or *The Rocky Horror Picture Show* (which, although Russell himself was not involved in its making, is nevertheless the greatest Ken Russell film ever made.)

I did, however, warm right away to this audio version of Sandy Wilson's ebullient lavender entertainment. I had all the melodies nearly down by the second time I heard them. Then the big decision came. Yvonne said you had to prepare an audition piece, practice it as though you were going to go out on stage in character in a real performance of the show. Now, which song?

There's a character in every song with a tale to tell, Yvonne told me; you turn yourself into that character, find out what she has to say (which isn't always in the words) and let her say it her way. I chose "You Are My Lucky Star." Twiggy's little sighing voice made it so appealing on the tape. Now here was a role that wouldn't be much of a stretch. Where's your Pierrot, *indeed.*

I found the right voice for it. I crooned myself to school, to and from classes and between puffs of cigarette on the patio before mom got home. I found a way all my own to do that song, blissful and liquid and warm. I recreated my old Dippity-Doo look from freshman year and wore my Thirties-style blue crepe blouse. I curled my lashes; if I'd known how, I would have beaded them.

After school I went to the choir room and waited for my name on the list. And I found out something I hadn't realized before, that Lads was full of incredibly cute, small girls who made perfect flappers, with really adorable voices, all cooing "I could be happy with you." I hadn't anticipated, either, how thin and wavery my own voice could sound, straining to be heard in a big music room, with a piano beside it trying to thump it into oblivion. The worst thing was, I discovered I'd prepared an audition piece that didn't exist.

"It's not in any of the music," the mother who played the piano accompaniment said.

"I don't think it's in the show," said someone else.

Everyone looked, in the piano score, in the Samuel French booklets, everywhere. No one could find it. Damn it! This was what came of watching all those Warner Bros. suspense thrillers and neglecting my MGM musical education! If I'd seen *Singin' in the Rain* (or, for that matter, had had the original *Boy Friend* album with liner notes, instead of that bootleg tape), I would have known that Russell had interpolated a couple of non-Wilsonian numbers borrowed from the Arthur Freed catalog. Oh, hell, so I had to sing "I Could Be Happy" all unprepared. I got red and damp and it was all I could do to get through just one chorus. They didn't ask for another.

They gave me the job of ripping sleeves and flounces off some costumes left over from *Little Mary Sunshine*, and stitching gold fringes along the sawed-off hems. I was supposed to get credit for this towards the Maskers, our school theater club, but that was meaningless outside of Lads. Because she went to public school, Yvonne had belonged to the Thespians, the national student theater organization; they had real competitions where they gave out awards and T-shirts. Yvonne got to go to one of these theater meets; she'd met her first real boyfriend there.

* * *

One night Natalie informed me she was no longer a virgin. You had *sex?* I said, amazed.

No, there was no penis involved. Then you are still a virgin, I said. Natalie said she was not.

Then how?

Natalie sighed and went very slowly, so I could catch up. "We were doing the thing called finger fucking, okay," she said, "and he got rough and I told him be careful but it was too late. I had white shorts on and I had to run in the back so mom din't see me."

Up till this time, I had been used to thinking of these things in terms of the baseball analogy, first base, second base, and so on. But that's a male method of assessing sexual experience. This was my first inkling that among females there is a far subtler and more advanced understanding of degrees of sexual advantage. There is of course also a far less impersonal standard for measuring sexual violation. It has something to do with the repercussions of sexuality, which are far more potentially horrific for women in every way, but even more with our reproductive physiology. The male locus of excitement, being limited to the tip of the primary sex organ, once aroused, experiences sexual sensation in only two modes: relief when he gets off, or frustration when he doesn't. He's a tap demanding to be turned on, and whatever it takes generally involves no more than a twist of the spigot.

But because a woman's erotic receptors are generously distributed throughout her body and intermingled with the workings of so many other vital organic systems, she experiences every sensation, whether externally or internally generated, as a completed act, so to speak. This is why women can neck for hours and hours and still push away a man's hand when he tries to steal one of those bases his fingers have been tingling for all night. Also why they can read books and books full of the most lubricious sex scenes, or lie in bed at night watching the most intriguing films, without having to physically relieve themselves from the excitement. The excitement, you see, is pleasure itself to us.

Which is why Natalie and I were as thoroughly ruined now as either of us would ever be.

*　*　*

One wonderful thing about Lads was nobody else wanted to be film critic on the school paper, *The Ladder*, so I had absolutely no competition. The woman who taught journalism, one of the ones who wasn't a nun but a real teacher, was obliged to give me Bs and Cs since I tended to go crosseyed whenever I tried to write a straight news story or take a current events quiz. But understanding the strengths within my limitations, she gave me generous leeway with the moving image beat. If I wanted to do a piece on the Academy Awards telecast or Sir Graves or my favorite Oscar Levant movies, I just typed it up in *Ladder* style, one column wide with a ragged right, and it went in as it was, spontaneous, unedited.

Mostly, though, I wrote about current theatrical movies. I would choose an interesting-looking film the Saturday before my deadline and have mom drop me off at the early show. Usually I'd stay to see it twice, which is a much fairer shake than I've been able to give most films I've reviewed since. In the case of the inscrutable *Three Days of the Condor*, I stayed not only for the 1 and 3 o'clock showings but for the twilight show as well. I never did figure it out, but I love Max von Sydow so there was no pain there.

In the case of *Mahogany*, I stayed to see it twice not out of professional integrity but awe. I already had a well-developed appreciation for what would later be termed the psychotronic style in film, and the abysmal glamor of an agonized Anthony Perkins gnawing on Diana Ross's reluctant bosom must needs be witnessed more than once, if only so you'll know you didn't dream it.

This really is an issue in film appreciation, the need to verify what you think you saw. There was a wonderful place called the Cabaret Cinema on Eight Mile Road in Southfield, near my dad's old bachelor apartment. It had been an adult movie house, and would be again, but for a few gorgeous years of my young womanhood it was the best revival house in my part of the continent. Here are some of the things I saw there:

Zardoz
My first Betty Boops
A Night in Casablanca
The Maltese Falcon (uncut—at last, it made sense!)
A Boy and His Dog
Reefer Madness
Creature from the Black Lagoon and *It Came from Outer Space* (both in 3-D)
The Magic Christian
Magical Mystery Tour
Start the Revolution without Me
And Now for Something Completely Different

And, most crucially, *The Rocky Horror Picture Show*.

Yvonne had seen *Rocky Horror* at college, at the only little first-run commercial cinema they had on campus. She and her friend had gone one weekday afternoon and had been the only ones in the audience, which made the experience even unrealer. They came back trying to tell everyone about it, and no one believed them. "They're all dancing up on this stage—in fishnets! And there's a guy in a wheelchair—in fishnets! Then they all jump in the pool—it's got Michelangelo's *Creation* on the bottom—"

"You were HIGH," everyone said.

Yvonne took me to see it for the first time—my first time—when it came to the Cabaret, while she was home on spring break. We had the theater all to ourselves. It was fate. I cannot remember seeing any film under more optimum circumstances. It was a beautiful print, with crystalline, lushly saturated colors. The Cabaret had a fine sound system, too. We took in *Rocky*'s Russellesque splendors in tranquil reverent silence, the last time ever such a thing was possible. The fad for turning *R. Horror* screenings into puerile rice-throwing megillahs would soon bore even into the Cabaret.

It seemed to me everything I'd been feeling all those years was in that film: the minatory, ecstasy-engorged life of my soul, set out in sequins on the screen. The lusts simmering under the surface of those old films that had been secretly exciting me all those years had been drawn up by the ingenious makers of this film, as though someone had stabbed the monochrome surface of the 1934 *Black Cat* and brought forth a gout of deepest arterial rouge. And that Karloff in fishnets, Tim Curry, that thunder-thighed siren in red lame bustier, with the hair and deportment of Joan Crawford and voice of Charles Laughton, gave mouth-to-mouth to something that had been suffocating in me, that startled me with its sudden full-throated violence. My gratitude to this daring and generous actor can never be expressed properly. But art does this for us, gives us what we never knew we needed.

I was led away dazed by my grateful sister, who was reassured that she hadn't hallucinated it after all. I was glad she was there, too, for my own affirmation.

*   *   *

I never paid much attention to things that were special to the Catholics. There was one day, for instance, when I'd missed the bus, and ran all the way to school, thinking I was late. But when I got to Lads there were no buses out front, and no other girls inside. I went to the office and the secretary told me school was out that day. It was a holy day of obligation. She asked me to call her when I got home, so she'd know I was all right. I was both indignant and touched by this aspersion on my sanity.

Again, not being one to pay attention to Catholic things, it took me by surprise when I came to school to find out there was no school that day, that we would all be going to the Mother House to see Our Lady of Fatima, and then after that we would all go home. Apparently what we would see would be so impressive we'd need the rest of the day off to deal with it. I managed to pick up enough information as we filed over to the Mother House to catch up with the occasion by the time we got there.

Our Lady of Fatima was an alias of the Virgin Mary. Apparently she sprang up on some little children in Portugal during World War I and told them, among other things, that the Russian Revolution was going to happen. Afterwards, the children gave a good enough description to an artist that a likeness could be sculpted, and this statue had been seen on occasion to cry real human tears. The weeping sculpture became known as Our Lady of Fatima, and was now on tour, sharing its miracles with the whole free world. Although nobody explicitly came out and said it, the statue's tears were given to be testimony to how horrible Communism was, and so Fatima was big with the sisters at Lads and the Polish community of Prague at large.

That day I wasn't with Natalie for some reason, but sat with my friend Ruthie, who I learned that day wasn't Catholic either. She was Lutheran, although, she told me, since her people were "carnies" (they operated one of the midway game concessions with a traveling carnival company), she ordinarily wouldn't be allowed through the doors of a church. The Catholics are so much more inclusive; it's part of their enduring popularity.

The ceremony in the Mother House was just another mass. Fatima was up there to the left of the altar, really nothing special to look at, just like something you would see in a furniture store window in Hamtramck. I kept looking, but it did not cry. Ruthie and I played tic tac toe in our pew as the others chanted, raised and lowered and crossed themselves.

There was something bad about this. Usually I took care to be more respectful in church. But this business with Fatima irritated me. Had I been the only one awake that day in Scripture class, or had I been asleep and dreamed the words: "You shall not carve idols for yourselves in the shape of anything in the sky above or on the earth below"? I mean, was this chapter and verse not intended to forbid the worship of inanimate objects? Wasn't this Betsy Wetsy statue just another damn Golden Calf? I sneered to myself, as Ruthie yawned discreetly, smiled, and hashed out a new playing field for us on the back of her prayer booklet.

At last they were through with their boogedy-boo, and we were let out. They had all sorts of tour paraphernalia in the lobby, so you could appropriate the magic of Fatima in exchange for a small donation. I took a white plastic rosary that looked as though it might glow in the dark and a medieval-looking long brown string with stiff cloth tabs on either end. The Lady of Fatima had told the Portuguese children to pray the rosary and wear this special string under their clothes, to keep Communism away, I suppose. I imagined what those hard little tabs would feel like next to the skin, and what they would smell like after extended wear. Being unauthorized to use them, I really had no business taking them in the first place; certainly not without paying for them. I later hid them in the underpart of my jewelry box, and never tried the rosary to see if it glowed. No use calling down a curse on myself.

*   *   *

Before she went to modeling school, Natalie had worn her hair plain and straight in a shoulder-length shag, sort of the way I was wearing mine around this time. But now she curled it every day, sometimes doing it up in pigtails with ribbons or colored yarn. This wasn't an improvement to me. I couldn't imagine why she would want to look so little-girly.

The Beatles had been broken up for a few years by this time. Yvonne had all the John Lennon albums that had come out since then, a George Harrison with sitars, and some of the better Paul McCartneys. Natalie had the latest Ringo Starr, something Yvonne wouldn't have touched with a pooper scooper. It had a song on it that would become her signature theme for that year, "You're Sixteen." That line about ribbons and curls, I suspected, was what was behind this regressive transformation in Natalie's hairstyle. But why would she want to be attractive to someone like *Ringo?* On the same record he said he was thirty-two!

She had a Sweet Sixteen party. I was invited, and so was Joy, a new friend of hers who went to public school, and her friends from the neighborhood Peggy and Denise. We all brought over our sleeping bags (everyone had them in those days, even if you never went camping) and bathing suits. I was glad it was a pool party because I hated the clothes I had come in. Everyone was wearing something cute except me. I was wearing a new short-sleeved rugby shirt that fit very tightly, which was how you were supposed to wear them, but it made me feel beefy. It was a relief to be able to change into my swimsuit, also new and tight, but in a rather more advantageous way. I relaxed and started to blossom, and as usual when I blossom, people came to me and started saying the most appalling things.

The Terabians had one of those blue plastic pools, not big enough to swim in (fine with unathletic me), but just deep and wide enough for a game of Marco Polo followed by a nice group soak. We went in just before twilight, and as the shadows deepened Natalie began to giggle and get suggestive. Bobbing on either side of her, Peggy and Denise gazed in amazement as the disembodied bottom half of Natalie's bikini floated past their chins.

Then as the birthday girl, no longer in her birthday suit, and her other friends dried off and went into the house for pop, I found myself sitting clammily on the picnic table, having a strange conversation with Mrs. Terabian.

It was in some ways similar to a conversation I would have later that summer with Mrs. De Groot. By then, I was feeling very angry about what was happening to Natalie. I said to Mrs. De Groot, don't you think these men are exploiting her?

Well, men will use you, but there are some women who like it like that, said Mrs. De Groot. Nobody's making them do it. They think it's great.

Mrs. Terabian took it a bit farther.

"There was a woman I worked with," she said, "who thought she was real popular with all the guys at the office. And you know what she did? She gave them all blow jobs."

I was chilled. I understood the message I was being given. No, I didn't. What I thought she was saying was what Mrs. De Groot said, that you shouldn't use your body to try to get men to like you. That meant nothing to me. Of course I wouldn't! I thought crossly. I don't want them to like me anyway!

But now I think what Mrs. Terabian tried to tell me in the creeping darkness next to the pool was: don't think you can play your own game. They make the rules. You call yourself a free spirit or feminist or whatever, and plan to take your pleasure with them on your own terms. They will see you coming. There are rules you never knew existed, until they're enforced.

Peggy had something to say to me, too. She caught me at seven the next morning, while the others were still deep in their bags. I was having a dreamy breakfast of Doritos. We never had anything remotely like it at my house; my mother didn't consider anything Mexican to be food. The unfamiliar spices that clung to my fingers as I raptly nibbled each crisp orange triangle were having a lovely effect on me, like a mild Spanish fly.

Peggy was a fat friendly blonde girl. Her mother was the Balkan war bride.

"I'm just glad to see Natalie has friends like you now," she told me. "I remember a couple of years ago I felt so sorry for her. She was this skinny little weird kid and nobody would play with her."

* * *

You dialed three numbers. Not any three numbers; not 911, of course. But for instance 364 would get you in. You would hear a shifting, phasing static sound, and the voices shouting around it: "What's your number!"

I had heard about it in junior high. They called it Pipeline. It was a glitch in the phone system that created a sort of party line that anyone in the area code zone could connect with. Since too many voices screaming at once would make it useless, the protocol was that you waited your turn until the couple currently trying to make contact had managed to get a phone number across and agree to hang up so one could call the other. Then you could start yelling "Hello!" yourself till you got someone of the right sex, and then "What's your number!"

I liked the idea, but just the technology of it. The couple of times back in junior high that I had tried calling guys from Pipeline (I would never give out my own number; I remembered the Jerry Booth guy) disillusioned me. The first one was terribly dull and lived in a trailer. The second one turned into an obscene phone caller, describing with gusto what he was going to do to me when we met, the scenario in his mind climaxing with a piece de resistance of thrusting his penis into my rectum. Why do you want to do *that*, I said, isn't that what homos do? That more or less ended the conversation, and that finished my Pipeline experiment.

These guys I had talked to were well into their twenties. And though age was no barrier in my mind regarding how I felt about Claude Rains or Vincent Price, I was not terribly interested in the sort of older man who would pursue a girl my age. The man I had in mind for myself would want a woman who could at least legally buy her own cigarettes.

Pipeline was how Natalie was starting to meet a lot of her men friends at this time, notably Kenny. For all I know, Kenny was one of the men I had talked to. What I thought at the time was, why would Natalie be doing such a kid thing? Pipeline to me was something like Charm Pops or menthol cigarettes, that you have a pubescent fad for and then get over. Anyway, what was the point of being as good-looking as she was if you had to meet men anonymously? But Natalie was moving so much faster than I was, her reasoning blurred for me.

*   *   *

Natalie never seemed to mind that I hardly ever invited her over to my place. It was understood that her house was better. There was nowhere to walk to in my neighborhood, except the Church Block and a couple of strip malls. There were no neighbors around to talk to, no good party stores (the ones with cigarette papers, lots of single beers, and clerks that minded their own business), no good parks (the kind you hang out in, not the picnic-and-softball kind.) Also there was my mother. Although I had plenty of privacy when I was on my own at home, this changed when I had a friend there.

But when I finally felt I must do my social duty, and invite Natalie to stay over, it was with a cautious, uneasy feeling that this evening would not be a success. I had made plans for entertaining her, bought ice cream, got out my Ouija board and so on, trying to remember all the things that used to go over well with my slumber party guests in sixth grade. But I knew I could just forget about that the minute she walked in in her short shorts and high-heeled sandals, sniggering and whispering to me that she'd make a date for us to go out with Kenny and a friend of his that night.

Natalie's mother had talked to my mother earlier that day, however, and so my mother told Natalie right off that as long as she stayed at our house she was to stay in. That was all right with me. I'd been listening to descriptions of Natalie's dates, and they didn't sound that tempting to me. But Natalie did not want to listen to records, and she didn't want ice cream, and she didn't want to communicate with the dead. She wanted to go out and see Kenny.

To have one's hospitality accepted only as an alibi—to open one's home to a friend, only to have it used as a jumping-off point for a questionable assignation—that's a wounding thing. I sat with nothing to do while my guest locked herself in the bathroom with her overnight case and put on the outfit she'd planned for that night: white denim cutoffs, a little pucker-cotton midriff top, gold sandals, and fresh ribbons. She made up carefully with her portable vanity lights in evening mode. Then she took me aside and told me I was to tell my mother we were walking to the drugstore. She could phone Kenny from there, and I could come along if I liked, or just go back by myself.

But my mother wouldn't even let us out the door. I was furious. At least if I had gotten Natalie out, I could have gotten rid of her. Now I was stuck with this thing that wasn't my Natalie anymore, that couldn't see me, couldn't hear me, couldn't respond to anything except this embarrassingly obvious urge of hers. Finally, Natalie said she would like to just go home. So, gladly, we put her in mom's car and delivered her back to Mrs. Terabian. Let her be her own daughter's zookeeper. It wasn't even dinner time yet! Well, at least with Natalie gone I could watch The Ghoul.

The Ghoul was a recently-introduced horror show host, a Cleveland-based rival to Sir Graves Ghastly (whom he referred to as Sir Greasy Gravy). He wasn't a ghoul at all, making no pretense of undeadness or love of morbid things, but a sort of ebullient low-grade Ernie Kovacs, improvising bits of mad comic business accompanied by snippets of old rock novelty songs. Occasionally, he'd jazz things up by setting fire to something or blowing it up. Watching the Ghoul made up for all those years I'd spent away from boys my own age; here, at a safe distance, was the adolescent male libido at work.

* * *

I was old enough: it was time to learn to drive. Lads didn't have a driver's ed program, but you could learn free through the public schools.

The closest I had ever come to operating a motor vehicle up to this time was when I was a very small child and my friends and I would pretend to drive to Cedar Point in our parents' cars (which of course weren't turned on at the time). Actually, driving a car was as foreign an idea to me as going to Cedar Point was. When I rode in a car, I looked out the window or at my lap, not at what the person driving was doing. As socially isolated as I was, I had no idea how extraordinary this was for a kid my age. Every other child in southeastern Michigan had been encouraged by a parent or uncle or cousin to try taking some car, truck or snowmobile out for a supervised spin. But I didn't find out about this initiatory custom until my first day in the field in my first driver's ed course.

The car had been started and the rest of the class and the driver rearranged themselves so I could get in the driver's seat.

"Okay, now shift it into reverse," said the instructor. I reached for the turn signal lever. The whole car reared back in laughter for five minutes.

No one could BELIEVE I didn't know where the controls were. No one could get OVER how puzzled it made me when I pushed the brake and the whole car jumped. "Pump it!" they shouted. I pumped it—it just jumped faster.

They made you do stuff in the driving simulator, which was like an amusement park ride that wasn't amusing. You sat in a fake partial automobile interior, rather like those used in studio-era films with rear projection to create the illusion of actors riding or driving, and manipulated the turn signals, the shift lever, the wheel, and pedals in synch with a film projected in front of you. When the film was about to turn left, you had to signal left. When the film veered around a corner, you had to veer exactly as it did. I was constantly running the simulator off the road, into trees and other cars, and never signaling the right direction.

THE PETER LORRE COMPANION   71

Film actually played a huge part in the Prague public school driver's ed curriculum. Not only the simulator films, but the ones they showed you in class, which seemed to be designed not to show you how to drive, but to frighten you out of driving. I was stupefied to learn from these films all the ways you could get killed in a car. Not just obvious ways like driving drunk or too fast, but by hydroplaning, or having your hood fly up suddenly so you couldn't see anything, or even being too tired, like the man in one of the films they showed us. He was coming home from a fishing trip, and dozed off at the wheel. Later he woke up in bed, feeling an awful discomfort in his legs. "But that's often the case, they say," the man said in voice-over, "when your legs have been . . . AMPUTATED!" Pan down his hospital-bedded body to the blanket where the lump made by his torso abruptly flattened into nothing.

It was a corny old black-and-white educational short, easy to laugh off if you thought rather than felt, but it had a dreadful effect on me. Not only was I absurdly inept at the wheel of my student car, but I was now timid and flinching as well. The laughing stopped; my partners in the student driver car were growing impatient with me.

"I'm not going to pass you," my driving instructor said one afternoon, with a grin that devoured defecation. What fun, to flunk a teacher's kid. I walked home and told my mother sadly that she was going to have to keep carting me around for a while longer. She said she really didn't mind.

* * *

Natalie called me up, with that rich, pleased giggle in her voice, letting me know she was calling me from bed. It wasn't her bed.

"Well, how you doing," I said. (Well, what do you say?)

"Mmmmmm, heh heh, fiiiiiine."

I found something or other to chatter about, then realized there was silence on the other end.

"Hi," she said a moment later. "Hehn-hehn hehn. Sorry I couldn't say anything for a minute there, cause."

I was being cued. "Why not."

The sticky giggle again. "I was just making Kenny feel good."

"Well, I won't keep you, you're busy," I said.

"Yaiss, well," heh-heh, "I'm getting this look now, I think I better go or you're probably going to hear something . . . isn't she . . . unless you wanna listen. . . ."

* * *

It was my special night. Mom would be gone till Sunday; she had gone on a mini-vacation with Mrs. De Groot to see the show at the Toledo Art Museum. Ruthie came to pick me up at 7 in a gold sedan with cream seats that was hers until her mom and dad got back from touring with the carnival. She had a little rubber frog on the dashboard that kept wanting to fall off. "Stay there, now," she said, sticking it back with a pat. "Mama loves."

We went to Westland to pick up Bridget, and from there to Canton for Nancy. Then to Plymouth, where Ruthie left us idling outside a party store while she bought a bottle of blackberry brandy. "Oh, Roothie, Roothie," she scolded herself merrily as we drove away from the setting sun towards Telegraph Road.

Telegraph lasted forever, and it was such a trip. It went down all the way to the end of the state, and every time you went on it you saw something you didn't remember from last time. If you turned left, it took you through the swankier eastern suburbs past the Machus Red Fox where Jimmy Hoffa breathed his last public breath, towards Meadowbrook, where you sat on the lawn with a champagne picnic and listened to the Detroit Symphony Orchestra. Turn to the right, though, and you went through Redneck Sodom. No-tell motels, all-night doughnut shops, the Pussycat Adult Movie Theater and other unspeakable loci of male entertainment.

The blackberry brandy was like the best cough syrup I'd ever tasted. This evening would mark the beginning of a recurring problem for me: I almost always have a marvelous time when I drink more than I should, but can never remember why.

I remember we stopped at a liquor store on Telegraph. Two rather attractive men with dark curly hair paused to talk to Nancy and Ruthie, who afterwards contemptuously referred to them as something that sounded like Camel Jocks. I thought they were maybe referring to the brand they smoked. Ruthie (who obtained our refreshments that night, as she had a fake I.D.) had gotten a bottle of something they called Mad Dog 20-20, which was like the worst cough syrup on earth, but interestingly had a Star of David on the label. At this point we needed a pit stop, so we pulled up at Ruthie's house in Dearborn Heights. It was a white cube on a small lot, a few doors down from a little clapboard church that presumably kept its doors chained shut whenever Ruthie and her people were around.

Ruthie's house was dark, wood-paneled, less like a normal house than somebody's summer cottage up north. There was a moist, woody smell there as in a vacation cabin that isn't regularly heated. There was no dust, but it looked like a place that ought to be dusty, with its soft old cushion-covered chairs and sofas, little framed pictures and mottoed plaques, whatnots cluttered with tiny glass and china morphodites. One wooden divider in the den was fitted with dozens of little shelves that held hundreds of miniature liquor bottles, all of them full. We didn't need to tap them; we'd finished the sabbath wine and were already into the peppermint schnapps.

While we took turns taking our ease, someone put the Foghat album on Ruthie's stereo. "Fool for the City." That song got to me that night. I want a city, I thought, with sudden urgency. Not just a bombed-out parking garage like Detroit; a real one. I'm going to *get* one, I told myself.

Then back in the sedan, and we went bummeling down Telegraph again. Cars full of boys chased us; we chased them. We stopped at a motel where Nancy said her boyfriend was. We woke him up but he'd been sleeping in his t-shirt and boxer shorts so he was decent. He seemed unfazed and rather pleased, coming to in a room full of frisky girls. He was maybe about twenty, with short dark military-style hair; he worked as a security guard and lived here in this motel, which I hadn't known you could do. We stood there in that dark room—he hadn't bothered to turn on the light—while Ruthie told us about the film she had recently seen. *Everything You Always Wanted to Know About Sex but Were Afraid to Ask.* Her favorite sequence had been the inaccurate fifties science fiction film parody with John Carradine.

"This big tit! It kills people—"

It was much more funny the way Ruthie told it than it is in the actual film, but then early Woodys are like that. He was still thinking like a scriptwriter, not a showman, so his stuff was much better conceptually than in actual execution. "Seizes henchman and smothers him with a large cheese" or "Giant breast rampages through countryside, obliterating people with lactal squirts" must have made you die when you read the treatment. Eventually Woody gave up on visual thinking entirely, and just wrote really talky movies, hiring great cinematographers to make them interesting-looking. We work in the dark, we do what we can.

After our visit with the security guard, the next thing I remember is parking somewhere along Outer Drive, passing around a joint. Bridget was crying because she was going out with a nice guy and felt terrible about it. There were things she did before she met him. "Finger fucking," she sobbed. The other girls assured her she had nothing to regret.

"My boyfriend last summer wanted to try it dog style," Ruthie remarked bemusedly as we sped back to Prague with my head in her lap. Nancy must have been driving them. Because they told me later she'd been doing it, even though she didn't have a license yet. That's really the only part of that evening, I think, I really can't remember.

When I went to get back into the house, there was a pouf of ribbons and purple paper in the door, and a card: "You're sixteen, you're beautiful. Happy Birthday! Natalie."

It was big and flat and square. An album: which one? As a rule, children give the gifts they would choose for themselves, so it wouldn't be the new David Bowie. Come, bu-bu-bu-baby.

It was Jefferson Starship. Okay, I would never play it. But it would be kept with love. I took out *Ziggy Stardust*, put on "Moonage

Daydream," lay alongside the Magnavox cabinet, and watched the walls revolve, glad that my mother wasn't home.

*　*　*

They buried Brecht with a knife blade in his heart. Good! I hope steel works as well as a pine stake. I would hate to think of him roaming the earth in his smelly leather jacket, floating into young women writers' windows, mesmerizing them into turning out plays to later be performed under his name. He did enough of that when he was alive.

It's hard for any female to read about Brecht without loathing this foul Bavarian. But I have a special distaste for him. I think he was a pernicious influence on *him*. *He* apparently thought Brecht was the cat's ass, which I don't fault him for; why should he share my tastes? Raised in the dual Germanic-Jewish tradition of romantic reverence for those pretending to formal creativity, he was a sucker for anyone who played the guitar and professed a social conscience. He liked Burl Ives, too.

It was partly just gratitude. Brecht did give him what was probably his most impressive stage role, as Galy Gay in his 1931 revival of *Man's a Man*. He started rehearsing him around the same time Lang was using him in *M*. Interesting, the parallels between Galy Gay and the *M* murderer. (Who has a name, of course, it's in the script: Hans Beckert. But I always think of him as M, a little intellectual slip, the way some people think of Frankenstein's monster as Frankenstein or Jesus Christ as God.)

Interesting, the parallels. Both wide-eyed boy-men transformed by irrational, uncontrollable pressures into killers. Both, at the point of indictment for their crimes, impelled to deliver speeches in which they beg piteously for mercy. Brecht was so impressed by his performance as Galy Gay he procured a motion picture camera and made a film of it. (WHERE IS IT! If you know, write me at the address in the front of this book; also if you can verify the rumor about the English-language *M* he's said to have dubbed himself.)

When *Man's a Man* bombed, Brecht wrote to the papers to defend his star, declaring it was the audience's problem if they didn't get it. The actor had made brilliant use of Brecht's directorial choices, such as having Galy deliver his desperate plea to the firing squad not as though he were really in fear for his life, but as though he were a lawyer reading a brief. Brecht probably thought his "I couldn't help myself" histrionics in *M* were hopelessly culinary.

Both of them came to Hollywood to get away from Hitler. I suspect Brecht was jealous of his friend's success here: the money, the red hot mamas, the four houses each with its own Japanese gardener (until they were sent to detention camps). Brecht himself was rather a flop on Studio Row. Nothing he wrote for the U.S. market really caught on, and this was really due to his warped, haughty view of Americans; he could never understand us, any more than he could read a map of China. Well, if he couldn't support himself writing for Paramount or MGM, wasn't there some other way to get a little money out of this stinking rich Mahogonny?

He fed his little actor friend's fears that he was prostituting himself, betraying his talent, that his beautiful soul was being eaten by the cameras, then sold him a palliative: slip some of those filthy dollars you're earning playing undesirable aliens for the Brothers Warner to good old Bert! He'll write you lots of great roles!

One of the screen treatments Brecht wrote for him was about the Great Clown Emaël, a famous low comedian who was in private life a sensitive intellectual who loved good books. Something certainly calculated to get under the skin of *this* little clown, whom Eric Bentley describes as being unsettlingly eager to prove how well-read he was. It wasn't just that he was trying to prove he wasn't a stupid movie actor, one of those "cattle" Hitchcock liked to sneer about. He needed to dissociate himself from the characters he played in Hollywood and on the radio, the *M* clones, the lurking psychopaths, the degenerate foreigners. All right, he was foreign and sort of degenerate, but not like *that*. He was infuriated when people caricatured him as some kind of poodle-stabber; he averred, correctly, that he had never really been a horror film actor. Frances Drake reported that just before shooting began on *Mad Love*, he insisted that he be introduced to her before they shaved him bald for the part of the erotomaniacal tyrant Dr. Gogol. He wanted her to know he was really a sane, presentable boy with lots of hair. *No puede vivir sin amar.*

Aside from Emaël, Brecht dreamed up a few other choice parts for him. He plotted a screen treatment of *The Overcoat* (that name Gogol keeps popping up) with him in mind to play the doomed little clerk (I thought we were supposed to be getting away from typecasting here.) He also wrote a Broadway musical for him, a dreadful, meandering thing based on *The Good Soldier Schweyk*, which also had a part for Lotte Lenya in it. Thank God that one never hit the boards, at least with him in it.

It's a shame that he never really got back to the theater. It might have made all the difference for him. Karloff, also a victim of typecasting (though a more grateful one—it saved him from a life of driving trucks), augmented his periodically shabby film career with a virile stab of legitimate stage work. He did *Arsenic and Old Lace* on Broadway, although notoriously not in the Warners film version; why didn't the Bros. release *him* to do a season as Dr. Einstein, one of his all-time most adorable movie roles? Maybe he couldn't afford the pay cut going to Broadway would entail; he wasn't very good at money management, and probably needed a steady flow of Hollywood dollars to pay off pushers and blackmailers. He was after all a very sick man. Brecht might have been having him on about really doing *Schweyk in the Second World War*, maybe at this point his memory or physical stamina weren't in good enough shape for the rigors of theatrical performance. I read something once about how, during the shooting of one of his Moto pictures, he was so weak that in order to effect the illusion that he was strong enough to punch somebody, they had to rig up his arm with wires and fly it, like Peter Pan, into his opponent's face. Ugh!

I wish he could have been happier being among us. It was right around the time he died that Andy Warhol taught the world to respect and value American pop culture icons. He might have lived to have seen that Brecht was wrong, that there was something honorable in what he'd done out here in the desert. To give life to that weird archetypal character, fascinating enough for a generation of scenarists, producers and directors to figure out endless variations on it for him to play, was a formidable accomplishment. And as Jung tells us (and he must have read Jung), we turn our backs on our shadow-selves at our peril.

In Stephen Youngkin's inestimable (if bowdlerized) biography, it's mentioned that during the seventies his estate sued a breakfast cereal company that promoted one of its products with a little blue cartoon ghost that looked and sounded fetchingly like him. The estate argued that he wouldn't have wanted to have been remembered that way.

But his life was spent making sure he'd be remembered as nothing else.

* * *

Natalie drove me to a place on Telegraph, a two-story motel, maybe the same one that Nancy's security guard had lived in. I couldn't be sure. A place doesn't look the same at noon as it does at midnight. We had the day off, Natalie and I; it was a holy day of obligation.

I followed her up the metal stairs, along the balcony, and into the room. Inside were Kenny and his friend. One of them might have lived there, but I doubt it. They had every reason to want to be able to leave this place without a trace immediately after they were through.

With surprising swiftness, Natalie and the friend were on the bed making out. Kenny got on the floor beside me, where I was sitting, and looked me over.

It hadn't occurred to me that I had been brought here for the purpose of sexual intercourse. Not in this raw a fashion, certainly. Natalie, back on the bed, meaningly tossed her shirt a couple of inches away from me, then her bra, as Kenny softly asked the sort of things that type of man usually asks girls. He put my hand on the front of his pants.

One day in sixth grade, I was sitting in class with a friend, passing pictures back and forth. Daringly, I drew a naked man with a penis.

I showed it to my friend. She looked at it and laughed. "Okay," she said good-naturedly, "now draw a real one."

That stumped me. Other than the general cylindrical outline, I had no practical knowledge of its real configurations until the day when Natalie took me to Hines Park to show me a copy of *Playgirl*. She went through it with me, pointing out the good parts.

I was a little let down. It looked like something you bought at a joke store. I found myself checking to see how it was attached.

"Of course, none of these are hard," Natalie told me. That apparently made all the difference.

Yes, this was the real thing, firm and squirming under my hand. I said immediately I wanted to go home.

Natalie was too far into her pleasures by now to care as we left. She'd done what she'd promised to do anyway. So there was no more said about it, and Kenny took me to his low-slung rusty sedan and drove me home. I wasn't afraid. Though this was a risky situation to be in, I just sensed that Kenny would be willing to let me get away. There are situations in which it is good not to be so madly desirable.

As we came to a stop in my driveway and I got ready to make my exit, he asked for a kiss. I let him mush around in my mouth for a little while. No loss.

"Don't you want to go back now?" he asked. No.

Then he asked, "Did you ever think about making it with Natalie?"

He may have meant this as a dig, like are you a lesbian for not wanting me. But I was astounded that someone who didn't even know me, for whom I was just a generic schoolgirl, my newness being why I'd been offered to him, would even raise the notion that I could be so corrupt. It was almost flattering, and I really considered it.

I had spent much of the last few years focusing my thoughts on the mysteries of gratification, what made me feel it, and under what circumstances. I thought of all the things I knew lesbians did. Did I want to kiss her, finger her, lick her? Did I want to . . . well, just for experience's sake, maybe someday with somebody, but . . . *her?* And it came to me that for all her sexualness, Natalie didn't feel sexy to me. I looked at his eager, veiny face, and thought what a pleasure it was to disappoint him.

Anyway, I was certain I didn't want him. So I got out of his car, and no more was ever said about any of this, until now.

5. MY FAVORITE BRUNETTE

A little ray of sunshine had come into my life at this time. Valerie had been in public high school, but changed her mind and switched to Lads in mid-year of our junior year. We discovered each other where I met all my great friends, in religion class.

She was plump and sweet as a little paczki, with shimmering hair and warm tawny skin scented with Love's Baby Soft. She called me Tweet.

She went around with a pack of other pretty, good-natured girls, and though I never got involved with the others she considered me part of her group. She gave me funny little notes, shared her candy with me, made me sit with her in assembly. I didn't have to be quite as much on my guard with her, since she pegged me as a weirdo right off, even teasing me about it. She thought it was cute.

She was a kindred soul in a way she never knew. She was herself devoted to a man completely inaccessible to her, Elton John, who had recently come out of the closet in *Rolling Stone* and so was even less likely than the average pop star to set his sights on Valerie. She didn't care; she just enjoyed him anyway. She turned me on to the subtler aspects of this entertainer, so overfamiliar from the radio, especially the work of his lyricist Bernie Taupin. For instance, the dirty stuff. "Look at the 'young girls,'" she said, pointing out the album liner illustration to "All the Young Girls Love Alice," with its aging, well-heeled sapphists' sidelong oglings of a bedraggled teen-age girl. And she showed me the words to "Island Girl," which I'd always liked the sound of, but was I shocked to find out what was behind Elton's cleverly obscured diction! Naughty, bawdy. Feel her nails scratch your back like a rake, indeed. What nice little Lads girls were listening to these days!

* * *

Natalie called and filled me in on her latest adventures. I hadn't really been in touch with her since the Kenny affair, and so missed witnessing the buildup to these new escapades. She told me every-thing eagerly, happily; I just listened, saying hmm, as you listen to friends telling you their weird dreams. It wasn't that I didn't believe her. I knew these weren't fantasies, because Natalie didn't have fanta-sies; like Lorelei Lee, whatever ideas came into her head she just acted out.

Her latest was that she had hopped out of a cake at a bachelor party and danced on the table. After that she had gone off with the groom—she had been his present. She laughed stickily, telling me that. I didn't ask what she'd charged.

I assume she didn't do it as a favor. So, she was a pro now. But where did she get her assignments from? And who were these men she was moving among now, so proudly and with no fear?

* * *

Then Natalie told me about Bonnie.

She said Bonnie had come with her, the way I had, to Kenny, maybe to the same place. She said a lot not saying anything, in that way she had.

"I told Kenny to go easy on her, it was her first time, but—" she laughed through her coated teeth—"You know Bonnie's pretty little. . . . She was having a hard time walking for a while after that. . . ." Laugh, laugh.

I guess I was so good by then at not showing what I really thought that she didn't know how much this horrified me. I guessed it must be true, as Natalie wasn't the type to make anything up, and I had the evidence of my own visit to prove it was possible. But I had gone with Natalie just because I was in the habit of following her; why had Bonnie gone? I couldn't remember ever seeing Bonnie and Natalie together in a way that suggested they were friends. I myself was capable of anything, but Bonnie seemed so gentle and happy and ordinary. Whenever I saw Bonnie after Natalie told me this, she seemed to me to be her natural self, unchanged. Maybe it hadn't happened. Or it had, and it hadn't mattered, in a way I couldn't understand.

* * *

This was getting altogether too gamy for me. I was famished for some more civilized discourse, and Valerie had it for me. She wasn't a culture vulture, but she was smart. I wondered at how she could be so happy.

"I used to have a bad attitude," she said. "I just made a decision. I was going to change."

I usually made every effort, as soon as I had finished with one phase of my life, to stuff it down the memory hole before it could interfere with the next chance I had of starting over. Valerie, on the other hand, never seemed ashamed of anything she had ever done. If she thought something was cool, she didn't care what anyone else thought of it.

"My friend and I made these paper dolls in junior high once," she said. "Want to see?"

She found the box in her closet and opened it for me. Think of saving something you did in seventh grade till you were in eleventh. I hadn't saved anything from then, not clothes or playthings or people.

It was a whole class of students, an entire grade of paper seventh graders from an imaginary school (public, of course). They were done with colored pencil on typing paper, about three inches high each, with long flat tabs under the feet so you could stand them up like commercial paper dolls.

Valerie laid them out for me on her bed, telling me all about them. They were all different, and she and her cocreator had given each a name and backstory and, most significantly, a social status. These were all detailed in the accompanying documentation, written on looseleaf paper in Valerie's own round, curling hand, and somebody else's, presumably her friend's.

The popular dolls were the tallest and thinnest, drawn with the sharpest pencils in the most careful manner and the most attractive colors. From there on down the social scale the dolls were drawn in a less artful, more childish manner, from the pleasant-looking but plain "normal" dolls, among whom I guessed Valerie and her friend would have classed themselves, to kids nearer the dregs, who looked practically like baby drawings, ugly-colored scraggly or lumpy squiggly things. The druggies were just brown scrawls. Valerie smiled wryly as she adjusted each member of this little world of hers into its proper row. This girl knew her people; she and her friend had faced down the junior hell I had fled all those years ago, and recorded what they'd seen there, frankly and with devastating acumen. I sweated a little, waiting for myself to turn up on that bed.

*   *   *

Just as we finished junior year it was discovered that Natalie was going to have a baby. I don't know how far along she was, but Mrs. Terabian wasn't one to screw around. Before you could say "right to life," she had whisked her off to Sinai Hospital to have her fixed.

I never asked Natalie any questions. So I can't tell you whether it was a dilation and evacuation, or whether it was too late for that and they'd had to do a D and C. I don't know whether or not her family argued this out before they decided on it or had set their minds immediately on this course of action. They may have had this in reserve all along: if the worst happens, we'll take her to the Jews. But I cannot imagine Natalie asking for this, not after her little comic books and that slide show.

This was 1976. If you were an unmarried teenage girl and it became known you were pregnant, you were finished. You would be expelled from any school you were in, parochial or public, because nobody wanted you corrupting their kids with your pregnantness. That was a mercy, because if they'd let you stay the other kids would have tormented you so cruelly you and your embryo would have ended up in the river before you were out of your first trimester.

They still had unwed mothers' homes, miserable hatcheries where you sat like a caged hen waiting for your baby to drop and either die or be sold to strangers. You might never see your child again, or it could get into the social service records and come around looking for you to ruin your life, again. As for that wonderful tradition of black women having and keeping their illegitimate babies, that might be fine on the Mississippi Delta or Cass Corridor, but where our mothers and grandmothers came from that sort of behavior got you a shaved head and a kick out of town in the dead of night.

Natalie's mother told me she was worried about Natalie. She was sullen and slept a lot, and kept carrying the little white poodle around in her arms. I wanted to say, you have mangled your child's mind through your own hypocrisy. But I let it pass.

Couldn't she just go to confession and get it wiped off her record? I guessed not; they would have already tried that. What else might work? Too bad Fatima was out of town. Or wait.

I know this Dr. Sherameta, I said. Let me give you her number.

*   *   *

I loved to take the bus down to see Yvonne at college. I got to sit in the bus station in downtown Detroit, smoking as much as I liked, in the relative safety of the women and children-only waiting area. The bus proper was not itself very interesting as it passed through the cornfields, but I was always sitting next to someone who wanted to talk, offer me candy, tell me their stories.

Once, right before Christmas break, I got a chance to go down and see Yvonne in a student production of *Company*. The show, and the whole staging of it, were far too adult for me and I just didn't grok it at all. My complaint was, what's the point of having a stageful of people singing for two hours about heterosexuality to a guy who turns out to be gay? Yvonne had been the only thing I really liked in the show. Her star turn, "Another Hundred People," had been done quite unconventionally (as she always did things onstage), with a whisper of Weillian sprechstimme, very thrilling.

She also had to be in one of the weaker numbers, "You Could Drive a Person Crazy," the one that's supposed to be a parody of an Andrews Sisters swing number. I told her it would have been infinitely better if they had tried to make it sound like the actual Andrews Sisters. The orchestration was all wrong and they'd taken it too fast; it was more like the Bette Midler version of "Boogie Woogie Bugle Boy" than the 1940s original. Listen to "Rum and Coca Cola," "Don't Fence Me In"; those girls swung, and you can't do that at a gallop. They drawled and slurred a song with a legato heavy with coolth and implied horniness.

But Yvonne wasn't in the mood for my discourse on ancient jazz. After a strenuous six weeks of rehearsals and two thankless weekends on stage, here she was down in the Rathskeller (or Rat as they called it, the nonalcoholic bar in the student union basement), bursting with tears of exhaustion and discouragement. The night before she had asked Josh Gleibermann, the twenty-year-old composition major she put before all others, what he had thought of her performance, and he told her she sucked. Now I was starting in.

I'm sorry, I said. You really were wonderful. She looked at me like, yeah, right.

This is the horrible thing: when any man tells you you are of little worth, there is nothing any woman can do to counter this. I was the last person on earth to hoist her ego, anyway. I was the weirdo who had cost her points in prestige with her friends, who had read her diary and written rancid comments in the margins, who had destroyed her only tape recording of her greatest triumph, as Luisa in the Prague Theatre Guild's production of *The Fantasticks*, by obliterating it with Alice Cooper on *The Midnight Special*. But she was too loving a person to even hate me for it.

The organic pizza we'd ordered came. It was hideous, like squashed-flat wheat bread spread with raw tomato paste. The 3.2 beer mocked us with its saccharine fake-alcoholic sourness; we drank it more furiously, trying to feel it. If only this weren't a dry town.

"But you can't not do what you want to do just because some dildo says you suck," I said.

"No, that's the point," she said, dabbing her tears. "Anyone can say you suck. It doesn't matter how good you know you are. Anyone can just come up and knock the stuffing out of you."

We tried giving the pizza a gnaw, but soon gave up. I had punched Peter Frampton's "Do You Feel Like I Do" into the jukebox, and now it was into its climaxing vamp, with that eerie talking guitar. "Loike Oi do." I wafted on its cool, obsessive rhythms, riding out my sadness and anxiety. Yvonne smiled a little wryly at me, so easy to please.

"What I feel like is like this quote I read once from Anne Sexton," she said, "where she said, what I really want is for people to stand around me holding up signs saying YOU'RE A GOOD GIRL."

Putting on our coats, we abandoned the shriveled, half-masticated pizza and exited the Rat. Maybe because we'd drunk enough 3.2 beer fast enough for it to have some effect before our bodies could eliminate it, we began to feel the spirit of the season. We went out into the unspeakable cold, with the moisture all frozen clear out of the air, which made the colored light garlands look like the satanic candle-jewels in a good print of *Tales of Hoffman*, and we sang, like sisters, like it ought to be done:

"*You could drive a person crazzzzzzzee. . . .*"

* * *

That was a rough winter and spring, the winter and spring of my senior year. What do you do when you can't drive and there's nowhere to walk to? When you're so bored you'll have your mother call in dead for you at school just because the Orson Welles *Jane Eyre's* on Bill Kennedy again?

Lucky Orson. He was an orphan. When he was my age he ran all over the world, working at the things he liked best, unafraid. While every move I made was clotted up with my dad and mom. The worst ghosts are the ones that are still alive. Not only that, I had to deal with my para-parent, dad's second wife, who had taken to whining at me about how difficult he was.

I had listened in silence too often; it had only encouraged these people, and now I felt overwhelmed. I went and told Valerie how blue I was. "Oh, Tweet!" she said sorrowfully. Her parents were going out that night, she told me; I should come over and she'd cheer me up.

So Valerie and I had a little party. She introduced me to the drink you make with whiskey and 7-UP, yum, and let me smoke cigarettes even though her parents didn't; they'll think it's my brother, she said. We got tipsy pretty quickly, and she started putting on Elton John records, a sure sign she was revved up. "Hello, baby, hello." "Elton!" I cried, spreading my arms. "Bernie!" she ran to them. We embraced. This was the first time I slow-danced with anyone.

I had her in my arms, her soft iridescent hair and babypowdered skin under my fingers. We hugged hard, stumbling round the kitchen. I felt her little nails dig into my back and scritch across, deliberate little minx. Wonderful.

Then we went to her bed, together, and clung blissfully. When had anyone ever held me like this? We kissed—I could feel her little wetness wanting to get through, but I pretended I didn't and kept my lips closed because I didn't want to go any further. I didn't have it in me to poke around. I wouldn't have known what or where or how, no instinct was pushing me. I felt pure joy just this way, and I intended it to last forever. We slept in each others' arms like golden princesses.

When I woke up it was horribly over. She pretended we were exactly what we were like before last night, and so I had to, too. Only it was very cold this time. Her paperdoll friend from junior high showed up (since when had she been invited to come over?) and they talked together as she made breakfast for us all. I duly received some French toast, said how good it was, got no response, and realized I was expected to go away now. I didn't even call my mother; I walked the three miles home, which seemed to take hours, because I felt so poisoned from all those sugared-up whiskies. And she hadn't even offered me the purple bag.

It was horrible now at school. She stuck with her other friends, who I hadn't known she was so close to. When I tried to talk to her it didn't work. I tried to make jokes and she thought they were pitiful. I called her one night and couldn't work up a conversation; it was like talking to Natalie, only I was being Natalie this time. "I just have nothing to say to you," she finally said. I hung up.

Now I was mad. If I'd done anything that had made her ashamed or resentful for having been taken advantage of, I could understand it, but I hadn't done anything! So if she was going to give me this fake-friendly coldness, smiling but cutting me, she was going to find out what I had in reserve, a little something I'd learned from my mother. "The existentialists say the worst thing you can to do a person is to refuse to acknowledge their existence," she told me. Try it: works every time.

So when Valerie would catch my eye and smile I'd look off to the side and pretend to be interested in something else. In our classes together, I'd deliberately choose seats out of her sightlines. Never another phone call. Of course, she didn't call me again. Nothing to say, right?

But then there was the day they had taken us all down to the skating rink, something they did periodically with the older girls to make us work off our excess libidinal energy. I was a horrible skater, too stiff even to fall down, and was taking one of my frequent time outs when Valerie came chirping up, hi, how ya doin, what do you think of this. I just said, "Sorry, I don't have anything to say to you," and stalked off like a Golem on my mechanical clogs.

Then Bonnie found me a few minutes later. "What did you do to Valerie? You made her cry!" Me? SHE was the one who started this. SHE was the one who turned into a popsicle overnight, leaving me to feel like a dirty old man over something that was her fault, if anyone's. WOMEN! What do they want?

There was an atonement. I slipped her a note saying I was sorry, and we were friends again, sitting and snickering together like always. You wouldn't have known anything had happened between us. But there was never another sleepover.

* * *

Now it was time for Natalie to be finished. By this point, even Natalie had had enough of herself. So her mother put together a team to do the job. There was the hairdresser that cut off her hair, and gave her a neat sort of pixie that made her look very clean, about three years older than I'd ever seen her look. Then there were the mothers of some other Kenny girls, who Natalie's mother had set about talking to in an effort to get to the bottom of his little business. "One of the things we've got to do is stop that Pipeline," said Mrs. Terabian.

You know, later that year, just for old time's sake, I tried dialing up Pipeline. It didn't work anymore.

Natalie really liked Dr. Sherameta. First thing after meeting Natalie, she immediately put her on birth control pills. Natalie said Dr. Sherameta told her it was natural for her to like sex, and if she wanted that feeling to feel free to help herself to her own body; she didn't always have to go to a man for it. She happily urged Natalie to really think about what she wanted, and what would be really good for her, and to make it a goal to fill her life with things that really satisfied her and gave her happiness. She listened to everything Natalie had to say with enthusiasm, and proudly told her what she thought she'd been doing absolutely right all along. Do what's RIGHT for you, Dr. Sherameta said.

Natalie told me that one of the things she learned at Dr. Sherameta's was how important friends are, "and that you are my dearest friend," she said.

I? The one you couldn't stand spending the night with without additional dong-laden company? The one who never says anything? That you don't even know?

But then, I'm the only one, next to Dr. Sherameta of course, who has heard about everything. The only one who was there as it happened. And never said a word, just watched. Perfect.

Besides, that was "dearest," not "best." It only goes so far, what I do for you.

* * *

Poor actors. It's horrible enough that an ordinary, nontheatrical person has to pretend so much in order to get through a life. Imagine doing it for a living, and most of the time you don't even get to write the script. They say he was fascinated by the word "creep," often used to describe the characters he played. Rightly so, as it was the single most evocative word you could use to summon up that ur-creature at the pith of those parts he so famously played, small, close to the ground, eugenically suspect. With that perverse whimsy of his, he devised means of turning that hurtful pejorative back at the people who used it on him. He would claim that he had studied the etymological derivation of the word (originally spelled *kreep*, he insisted), and discovered it had originally meant something akin to "fellow," "regular guy," "mensch," in other words, the opposite of its current connotation. However, it had been corrupted through ill-usage by careless native English speakers (how ironic, that this had to be pointed out to them by a foreigner with a funny accent). He'd go around calling people creeps, then declare that they shouldn't get mad at him; it was really a compliment. This "creep" business became a sort of Hollywood in-joke, viz. his cameos in the films *Meet Me in Las Vegas* and *Muscle Beach Party*.

He was a creature of paradox. Casting him as the child-murderer in *M* was a sort of sick joke on Lang's part, because he looked so much like an overripe schoolboy at that time; visually, he made a nice couple with his victims. The most famous signature of that particular role, the whistling of Grieg's "In the Halls of the Mountain King," wasn't even really him. He couldn't whistle. He just mimed it while Lang himself did it off-camera.

It's de rigeur mortis among the higher critics, the Lotte Eisner crowd, to say that the Hollywood showmen that employed him during his American exile were a bunch of insensitive oafs who destroyed him by typing him as the *M* killer, forcing him to endlessly reenact that one famous *tour de force* of mingled terror and pity and thus throwing away his potential (which he certainly had) to do so much more. But I don't know. As far as typecasting, if you look at some of the parts he played onstage in Germany before he even got the call from Lang, in *Spring Awakening, Happy End, Tales from the Vienna Woods,* they were all proto-creeps, little brothers to Mr. M. And if you read through descriptions of the film roles he did in the years immediately following *M,* the German film industry seemed well on its way to making him a forgotten footnote to cinema history before Hitler did him the professional favor of scaring him out of the country.

My feelings are mixed. I mean, a lot of the films they put him in here were terrible, which is why at this late date I've still only seen about half of them. It would take a higher embarrassment threshold than I possess to make it through *Hell Ship Mutiny,* and I've never had the guts to actually sit down and look at *The Big Circus,* though I'm sure watching him play a clown would be a fillip for jaded nerves. On the other hand, I sympathize with Hollywood, which was never set up to fulfill anyone's creative potential, but I think really did try with him. It was certainly extraordinary for anyone who looked like him, especially as *ethnic* as he did, to be allowed to work in that pantheon of Aryan beauties. There were obvious problems he might have corrected, like his weight and those terrible teeth (very naughty of him, in that land of grapefruit and cosmetic dentistry), that might have made them more inclined to take him seriously as a leading man. Though it was nearly impossible to make the baroque planes of that incredible face look conventionally handsome, even normal on film. Even the master Von Sternberg failed at it. There are some portions of *Crime and Punishment* in which he shimmers like Dietrich, and in others he just looks like a shoat. So having to watch him through the lens of a camera exclusively is a torture of Tantalus, glimpsing shades of that full beauty you know to be there, but never captured, never held for your own eye to satiate its longing self with, not in *your* lifetime. Excuse me. Mine.

*   *   *

Neil was one of my sister's friends. He was my age, in the same grade. When I knew him through her he seemed normal.

He was friends for a while with one of Yvonne's boyfriends, and till they had a fight and stopped seeing each other (Neil and the boyfriend) they would all come over and drag me along wherever they were going, because I never went anywhere and it bugged them. I saw the first drive-in movie of my young adult life in a back seat with Neil. It was *The Last Detail*. Yvonne and her boyfriend were in the front seat. These were the only people I've ever known who went to drive-ins to watch the movies, but then you would have to be insensitive to the point of psychopathology to neck through *The Last Detail*. I was petrified with depression afterwards. Neil cheered me up, though, by telling me stuff about Jack Nicholson. He told me his theory that in his famous cameo as Wilbur Force the masochistic dental patient in *Little Shop of Horrors*, he is actually doing an impression of Roger Corman. There is in fact a notable resemblance. "Oh my *God* don't stop *now!*" we shouted together, and suddenly looked at each other in delight.

Neil was the first person I'd known in six years, besides Yvonne and my mom, to whom I could talk about anything that really mattered to me for more than five minutes. Neil and I talked mostly about movies, but that was everything to me anyway. Men were usually so foreign to me, but here was a male I could talk to with more ease than any girl or woman, because no female I had ever met remotely understood why anyone would yearn to see *Strange Cargo* the way most people ache for their first act of coitus with a new beloved.

Actually, I was intimidated by him. He was slim and slight, borderline handsome, but this was thrown off a little by his mouth, which didn't have lips exactly, but curled back at the edges to reveal the inner lining in an off-puttingly clinical way. He also wore glasses that magnified his eyes like Percy Dovetonsil's, but he would soon get contacts, and from then on the young girls were going to have to look out.

After Yvonne left for college, he unspokenly shifted from being one of Yvonne's people to one of mine. Recently, he had started coming over just to see me. By the time I felt comfortable enough to go visit him at his house, his parents had moved him into the basement (as Prague parents customarily do with sons over seventeen who neglect to move out), which, with his natural instinct for organization, he'd made over into his private passion pit and professional headquarters.

Neil's red plush-carpeted lair had a classroom-style projection screen depending from its west wall. To the north were his bookshelves, loaded with film books he'd found at the used book stores in Ann Arbor or had never returned to the Prague Public Library. He chose well: Leonard Maltin's *Selected Short Subjects* (still one of the finest pieces of original film scholarship I've ever read), the script of *The Third Man*, Carlos Clarens' deathless testament of horror film history, Walter Kerr's *The Silent Clowns* (which I later purloined for my own library.) To the east was his bed, and in front of it a desk, where he kept an index file with every film he'd ever seen described in it, with a star rating, as well as a 16mm Movieola and an ash tray. Neil smoked regularly; his parents had given up trying to make him stop. He smoked Gauloises, because that's what Jerry Lewis smoked.

I still had a year to go of school at this point, but he was already through with it. I found this out one morning when I was off from Lads for yet another holy day of obligation, and he dropped by. I said isn't this a school day for you? and he replied that he didn't go there anymore. I asked why. He said, "I've learned everything they can teach me."

I thought this was a terrible mistake, to drop out. He ought to graduate so he could go to the American Film Institute or USC or UCLA film school like Coppola and Lucas and Jim Morrison. "I don't want to go to film school," said Neil, "I want to make films."

But nobody goes to film school to learn to make films, I said. If you don't already know, you don't belong there. You go there to make connections. But you couldn't tell Neil anything unless you were Jerry Lewis or Orson Welles.

To the west was the laundry room and an antechamber where a pool table was kept. Neil had that much of Hollywood in him already; we would go in and play for a while, till he got sick of slaughtering me.

But mostly there were movies. Neil always had something to show me. We were just on the edge of the home video era then, and it would still be a couple of years before Neil got his glommers on his first Betamax, so running films for ourselves was still a cumbersome activity. Neil and his friend Dave would go to the Dearborn Public Library, where James Limbacher worked. He was a librarian whose specialty was movies; he hosted an early morning telecourse called *Shadows on the Wall*, about the history of film, which I tried to catch whenever they ran it; it was great (there was even a clip from *M* in it.) Neil and Dave said he was really nice. They'd always come home loaded with cans of films he'd recommended from his library's rental collection. Neil and Dave would sit for days in Neil's basement doing nothing but watching Limbacher stuff. Mostly comedy at first, Buster Keaton, Laurel and Hardy, Chaplin. *The Sex Life of the Polyp*. But eventually they diversified into broader realms of cinema. The fundamental difference between the way they watched films and the way I was used to doing it was that while I was focused on what the films did to me, they were obsessed with finding out how they worked. If they saw something they particularly liked they would run it through the Movieola frame by frame: the *Psycho* shower scene, the jump cut where Anton Walbrook smashes/doesn't smash the mirror in *The Red Shoes*, the little sight gags in *Porky in Wackyland*.

If Dave hadn't existed, someone would have to have drawn him. He was small and round and big-featured, appealing in the classic funny-animal way, and he had this wonderful raspy-squeaky voice. Though he did everything possible not to be cute—growing a beard, indulging in neglectful hygiene practices—he was adorable nevertheless. I didn't see this the first time Neil introduced us. We were having lunch together, and I had never seen a human being eat mac and cheese quite in the way Dave did. But then Neil put a pad of paper and a pen in front of him, and for the next three hours we crouched over him in amazement, shaking so hard and wiping our eyes so that you would have thought we were crying.

It was inevitable that Dave would become a famous cartoonist. It was just a matter of waiting until he was not so ridiculously young, and had had time to produce enough of a body of work that was sufficiently beyond juvenilia to be published. This made him a perfect companion for Neil, who was intent on becoming Hollywood's belated answer to the French New Wave. You have to feel a little deferential in the company of that kind of aspiration.

Being the next Crumb/Avery/Bakshi/Welles/Lewis/Godard, it was natural they be united in their current endeavor, which was to do whatever they had to do to get out of Prague and go where life was really happening. This isn't to imply that they were the sort of brats who would spend the rest of their lives spitting on their wall-to-wall-carpeted, comparatively trauma-free suburban childhoods. I think every one of us, even when we were very young and restless, appreciated not having to grow up in some urban combat zone or bleak rural slum. But we were aware that Prague had been planned only as an optimum medium for raising us, not to accomodate our emerging adulthood. So we plotted to get out, and this wasn't rebellion, just natural ontogeny. When a chick has been hatched, it's not meant to stay under the hen.

* * *

Once, in an effort to open self-relevatory channels with an insecure man, I confessed to him the nature of the great love of my life. "But I thought he was gay," he responded.

What! I said, what have you heard! what do you know!

Nothing. I just thought he was, that's all.

Is it because of *The Maltese Falcon?* I asked. (Actually a rather subtle performance. Notice how most critics discussing homosexual themes in that film go on and on about what an old queen Casper Gutman is, when it's Joel Cairo who can actually be seen grabbing Sam Spade's ass.)

I don't know, he said crossly, but he is, isn't he? (This man and I weren't going to last long.)

If there is one thing I've learned in all my years as a remora riding on the shark of the film business, it's that you can never really know show people. Unlike the rest of us, the overriding concern of their lives isn't what they do, but how interesting they are doing it. You have to remember that whenever you hear a story about a celebrity, whoever's telling it isn't trying to tell you the truth; they're trying to tell a good story.

Here's an example. A certain person published a book a couple of years ago in which he claimed that Mrs. Lon Chaney Jr. reported having seen *him* put a cigarette out in his wife's face. (Which wife? Celia? Kaaren? Annemarie?) I wrote to this person immediately care of his publisher, whose sense of responsibility for its products apparently does not extend to fact-checking, and requested the source of this anecdote. I got no reply. I did, however, locate another version of this same story, only Mrs. Chaney Jr. was not mentioned, and it was one of the Korda brothers doing it to one of his wives (whether Merle Oberon or not, they didn't say). Which leads me to suspect this legend was fomented by some Hungarian Semite Defamation Society.

So I don't know. I hear there's a photo of him somewhere that shows him kissing George Raft in front of a group of horrified studio tourists, but that may not have been *his* idea.

I once told Dave a story I'd read in a memoir by one of Bogart's lovers about Bogart and him at some night spot in Rome, around the time of *Beat the Devil*. They were eyeing an ostentatiously-dressed woman whom Bogart thought must be some kind of aristocrat. But *he* said you're wrong, she's a pro. They went up and asked her, and she, flattered at this attention from two such celebrated men, admitted she was for hire.

"And then they took her upstairs," said Dave.

Well, the book hadn't specified.

Neil approved of my taste in this respect ("Chaplin said he was the greatest living actor"), but in general had no patience with my star fetishism. He was an auteurist, and set out to knock some sense into me regarding the real source of cinematic ecstasy. Not only in his basement, where I saw *The General, Modern Times, Can Hieronymus Merkin Ever Forget Mercy Humppe and Find True Happiness?* and other finds that Neil wanted to impress upon me, but at the Cabaret, on the rare occasions they were running something Neil hadn't seen or wasn't already sick of, and in Ann Arbor, where the ten or twelve student-run film societies on the University of Michigan campus had something going almost every night.

"Now get ready," Neil would tell me, going into *Touch of Evil*, "you're going to see the world's greatest crane shot." Or, coming out of *La Dolce Vita*, he'd explain to me about wide-screen frame composition. "Did you notice how that was panned and scanned?" he'd asked.

So that was why, in certain big films made in the fifties and early sixties, the camera would suddenly go *boing* across a huge blank space from one character to another. I had thought that was just a crappy kind of tracking shot. No, that was panning and scanning, another fraud perpetrated on the public. Like what Bill Kennedy did to *Casablanca*.

The first time I saw *Casablanca* on Bill Kennedy, my reaction was, "This sure is stupid and incoherent." I didn't make the connection then between the deformed narrative of the film I was watching and the fact that I was watching it on commercial TV. I should have known. Hadn't I seen what Channel 2 did that one time with *The Producers*, cutting to a commercial right in the middle of "Springtime for Hitler"?

Bill's butchers had taken out whatever chunks of *Casablanca* they'd felt would never be missed in order to shorten the running time so they could fit in all the commercials they needed to run during their show's two-hour time slot. So they eliminated the flashback to Paris, much vital exposition concerning the letters of transit including practically all of Sydney Greenstreet's role, and most of Dooley

Wilson as well. (Though Dooley had to go for censorious rather than commercial reasons. This was Detroit, after all, Race Riot Central. So "That's Why They Call Me Shine" hit the cutting room floor of Channel 50, along with the Abraham Lincoln blackface number in *Holiday Inn*, the Willie Best scenes in *High Sierra*, and the more egregious snippets of the "Little Rascals" shorts.)

Only when Neil dragged me to Auditorium A, Angell Hall, where the Ann Arbor Film Coop held its screenings, to see the uncut *Casablanca* at last, did I realize how unjustly I'd judged this film. Unmutiliated, it is a lovely thing, a cool, lush set of numinous white-gray boxes that you can crawl through for hours without slaking your longing for those sultry delights it seems to have waiting for you just off camera in every langorous setup.

But I don't love *Casablanca*. I watch those celebrated *Play It Again, Sam* scenes of petulant recrimination and noble renunciation under the ceiling fans and airplane propellers not with pleasurable romantic tears, but through a gauze of dull mourning. How could they bring him out, so soigne and cute in his white jacket and brilliantined hair (you can tell Bogart, for all the scripted contempt he was forced to express towards him, could hardly keep from bending over and rubbing his nose with his own), and then drag him off and snuff him with two-thirds of the picture left to go? To top it off they kill Conrad Veidt, too.

Youngkin says that before America entered the war he could often be found in his studio dressing room between takes, morosely listening to Hitler's broadcasts. During the shooting of one of his Moto pictures, his director Norman Foster (the one who had to wire his punching arm) came to call him back to the set. "The whole world is falling apart, and you want me to make a *picture!*" he retorted in disgust.

No one involved in the making of *Casablanca* thought they were doing anything special. It was just another rivet-and-bucket assignment for the war effort, like *Cross of Lorraine* or *Invisible Agent*, but it just happened to be assigned to an exceptionally talented group of creative people, who through true collective effort (take that, East

Berlin Bertie) created a spectacular piece of media weaponry to rival that other piece of lapidary propaganda, *Triumph of the Will*. As it turned out, the Warner Bros. beat Leni Riefenstahl all hollow.

Recently an acquaintance of mine invited me to a *Casablanca* party, a fundraiser for her Junior League chapter. I'd been a behind-the-scenes consultant for this affair, so I had to take a look. I got in costume and went by myself, slipping in around eleven-thirty.

It was gorgeous. They'd had the propitious inspiration of having it in an airplane hangar, which trebled the allusions to fundraiser, film, and movie set. They'd masked the bare walls with black velvet drapes, and dirty silvery light from the overhead lamps filtered down, making blacks and whites glow and washing out every color into a halftone. The gambling tables and bar, requisite for any Junior League function, fit the concept perfectly. The Leaguers themselves went with the decor, looking like subdued, wary refugees or dress extras in their white jackets and vintage gowns. In its unreality, it felt too real. I knew if I loitered there long enough *he* would materialize and come looking for me (I left early).

*   *   *

Neil was a tiger when it came to his viewing habits. You'd be lying around his basement cave and happen to mention that they were showing *Steppenwolf* with Max von Sydow that night at Aud. A Angell Hall at 7:30, but since it was already a quarter past seven you guessed you'd missed it. From Prague, Ann Arbor was a twenty-five minute drive. "We'll never make it," you'd say.

At 80 miles an hour down I-96, you'd make it.

Neil not only had a line on what was showing at all the Ann Arbor campus film societies and the Detroit Institute of Arts, but his ability to ferret out movie gold on TV was stronger even than mine. He introduced me to Elwy Yost, the preternaturally affable Canadian movie show host, whom I'd been missing all these years due to insufficient tinfoil on my antenna. Elwy had two shows he hosted on TV Ontario: *Magic Shadows*, a sort of really good *4 O'Clock Movie* without commercials, and *Saturday Night at the Movies*, which offered extraordinarily well-chosen double features from the whole spectrum of classic sound cinema, from Charlie Chan to Lina Wertmuller. Even if the films weren't something you were excited about seeing, the segments in between in which Elwy interviewed various directors, actors, critics, and other film-related persons were always good viewing. Elwy was a running joke with Neil and Dave; he was so exhaustively good-natured and enthusiastic about every single film and person he presented, and he was so ripe for caricature. All the features in his face, glasses and moustache and little mouth gaping with delight, were all squnched up at the bottom of his big bald head. Dave was always saying he was going to make an Elwy egg cup, with the face on the base. Neil loved to make fun of Elwy's resourceful way of always finding some topic to interview someone about to go with every film, e.g. *Of Mice and Men*: "Is it true you can kill a rabbit by hugging it?"

In a sense Neil was my first boyfriend (or first one since second grade), but then he didn't count. For one thing he was very shy with me regarding our personal relations. He did once or twice say that he wanted to marry me, in a little boy way, but when I would aggress and want to kiss he would go limp and patiently wait it out until I was through and ready for him to show me films again.

The truth was, he was a sentimental boy and didn't care to exert his heart or body on any female but the one true desire of his soul, which was Andrea Vale. I could certainly understand this. Andrea Vale was the one true raving beauty Prague had ever seen. She was screamingly feminine, rounded but delicate, lithe-limbed, with mahogany hair that hung to her shoulders in a sinuous bob. She had real violet eyes, big and round like an old-fashioned doll's, and palest pink lips that opened in a circle like those of an exquisite goldfish. I recall one afternoon back in junior high when she had sat next to me on the school bus, arms full of things, and said, "Would you do me a big favor?"

She held out a paper bag. "Hold this for a minute?"

I would do it—I would do anything. I breathed so shallowly all the way home that a mirror in my mouth wouldn't have clouded.

There was something holy about her, something like art, that was meant to be revered. And you knew a guy would look at her and all he'd think was—I was disgusted. I wanted to protect her forever.

Neil had written a movie for Andrea, or was still writing it, as his ideas for it changed and it had to be updated. He had actually shot some of it back when Andrea was still cooperating with him. Judging from the parts I'd seen, and the script he'd let me read, the gist of it was: A projectionist in a revival house discovers a print of an old film one day in the theater's storeroom and decides to look at it. It turns out to be a 1940s film noir with a beautiful girl in it, a real femme fatale in seamed stockings, ankle-strap platform shoes, and dark lipstick who stabs the film's hero with a stiletto. The projectionist decides to show the film at the theater, and while watching it over and over as he screens it for the public, falls in love with the femme fatale. Then one night, walking down the street, he sees the girl from the movie, wearing modern clothes and makeup, but recognizably the same girl. He follows her; she appears to be about to go into her apartment, but seems to change her mind, seeing him but pretending not to. She goes to a diner to talk to a waitress friend, glancing at him through the window. She walks through the park with him trailing her, a scary segment with Lewtonian overtones. She stops to talk to a policeman, and for a moment seems to be telling him about the projectionist following her, but it's a false alarm. She goes back to her apartment, through the window of which the projectionist watches as she sits in front of a television that's showing *Scarlet Street*. She goes to the mirror, brushes her hair, puts on lipstick and a pair of platform shoes. Then she goes out of the room, and he sees her through the doorway, going upstairs. He runs to the side of the building and starts climbing the fire escape. He catches glimpses of her on the stairs as he goes. Then he sees she's opening a door marked "To Roof." He clambers up on the roof, and she's there. He stands in the shadow by the door watching her. She stands there on the edge, looking down. Then she turns to him, smiles, and comes towards him. He's thrilled. But then the door he's hiding next to opens, and a handsome man comes out and she kisses him. The projectionist turns around and goes back to his theater. From then on he will show no film except the film with the femme fatale in it. He's fired, and stays home running the film on his own projector until he's evicted. Dying, clutching the final reel of his beloved film, he crawls back to the roof of the building where he last saw her, and expires, the film can falling from his hands over the edge of the rooftop, spilling open at the feet of the girl (again in her ankle-strap shoes) and her boyfriend, who kneels down and, taking up the end of the strand of film, pulls it taut to look at it. Fin.

Now Neil was reworking it again. He said there was a part for me in it now. He showed me some of it—I was driving a sports car very fast along an oceanside cliff. I realized he didn't know me very well.

It was very frustrating for Neil. Perhaps because he'd watched so much Chaplin and Keaton and Lloyd, "The Girl" was of paramount importance to his self-concept. After all, Charlie and Buster and Harold would basically just be psychopathic maladroits if it weren't for the character-driving warmth derived from their interactions with the likes of Paulette Goddard, Natalie Talmadge and Mildred Davis. To be sure, Neil had a more sophisticated attitude towards his muse. In his hopeful imaginings, Andrea was Anna Karina and he was Godard. But in real life, he could never even get to contempt with her. She said she thought of him as a friend.

I had a funny experience with Andrea Vale once. It happened after Yvonne left college for New York, but before things really started happening for her there. Andrea and Cherie Barrette were in town, and some other old high school friends of theirs and Yvonne's were also over on spring break. We had all gone out with three guys Yvonne knew. Andrea and Cherie, strawberry and champagne, were not merely the most gorgeous girls in Prague; they were dazzlingly smart. Rather than being cheerleaders, they exhibited themselves in more advantageous ways, doing drama and forensics. Andrea won a trophy for her delivery of a piece from Woody Allen's *Getting Even*, and Cherie scorched a statewide Thespians competition as Passionella in *The Apple Tree*. These girls were the berries.

We went to a disco, and Yvonne and I barely made it onto the floor, because it was so packed with guys dancing with Andrea and Cherie. The guys we'd brought with us just seemed electrified, amazed at being with these incredible girls, just as extraordinary in Manhattan as they had been back in Prague. Andrea and Cherie seemed equally galvanized at just being what they were. After all, they had only been world-class heartbreakers for about two or three years; they weren't entirely used to it yet.

Eventually, the two guys who were more average-looking dropped back to the table where Yvonne and I had been sitting there watching all this, and Cherie and Andrea kept dancing with the one remaining guy, Dan, who was not in their class but still the best-looking thing available that night. Dan was getting hot, clinging all over them, just delerious with pleasure. And they felt the same, you could tell.

The next morning Andrea and Cherie were over giggling about it, while the unobtrusively lovely Yvonne and her little sister dourly ate their granola.

"Dan was getting . . . really. . . ." Andrea was saying.

"Yeah . . . really. . . ." Cherie snickered.

Yvonne solemnly raised her spoon. "He's gay, you know," she said flatly.

"Oh, no."

Yvonne then started to tell them what she knew about Dan's established preferences.

Andrea and Cherie were flustered, downcast. They fluttered away. Yvonne and I grimly finished our coffee and trudged off to MOMA; I'd wanted to see the surrealists.

"The world doesn't just need artists," my mother used to say to me. "It needs audiences." She considered being an arts consumer an honorable calling. "I love art," she said, "because it's the most innocent thing a person can do."

Now critics are traditionally despised things; they are seen as lampreys on the trout of art. But to be a critic is a good life for a woman. Dorothy Parker, Susan Sontag, Penelope Gilliatt all made nice little careers centered on this specialty. You can think like a human being in the critical arena; you don't have to preen and please and make nice. You can flick your tongue and tell the truth and laugh in any face, and no one can harm you for it. (Unless, like Dorothy Parker, you give your boss' wife a bad review.)

Film semioticians, feminist ones anyway, always write about the male gaze. Well, I have eyes too. If a woman finds that she just doesn't have the urge to be watched, why not become the watcher? Watchers are wanted, especially by the 75 percent of the clinical population diagnosed with narcissistic personality disorder who are male, according to the DSM III. What good is an actor when there's nobody out there in the house watching?

Watching.

6. The White Demon

Occasionally I've had a recurring dream, something like the classic student's dream in which you know you've got to take a test, only you've never been to the class and don't even know which room it's in. (I've had that one too, but only after it actually happened to me once.)

In this dream I would be called on at the last minute to perform a major role in a stage play, musical, or operetta, only I had never studied the part. This unpreparedness would never frighten or intimidate me. I would put on the costume and go on, feeling perfectly comfortable, and ad lib my way through the part. This wouldn't bother the other players at all. The audience would roar with delight at me, and I'd be a smash hit star.

Cf. my audition for that year's Lads spring musical, *Fiddler on the Roof*. You would think they'd almost have to give me a part on the grounds of authenticity, though the most identifiably Russian-Jewish thing about me, my brown-black hair (which was almost down to my breasts now) would have to be covered with a kerchief if I were to play one of the pious Orthodox women of Anatevka.

But my ethnic right to be there didn't stand by me when I approached the music room the day of tryouts for *Fiddler*. I couldn't go in there. I got about ten feet away, then suddenly seized up and scampered back down the hall. By the time they called my name I was already home in my slippers watching Canadian children's programming.

You don't have to go on the stage. Isn't that wonderful? It's not like in a dream where you have to go. If they call you in real life and beg you to entertain them, you can tell them to stuff it and leave you alone. Leave it to the people who can't stand it unless they're up there, who genuinely care whether or not people are paying attention to them, whose egos are so big (or so small and surrounded by neurotic defenses) that they can't be embarrassed out of doing anything, so unintimidated by concerns about whether or not their performances are good enough that they can actually concentrate on *being* good.

When people have accused me of being what I am because I'm secretly envious of those people who "put themselves out there," I never say anything back, I don't try to challenge their cliched assumptions. How can they understand my particular deviancy, my wanting to *see*, rather than *be seen*? And that when I pick a performance apart, it's not out of jealousy, but out of frustration that I've been led on, then denied what I need? That what I seek is not revenge, but satisfaction? They can't understand; forget it.

The weird thing was that though I skipped the audition, I still got a part. They recruited me through the Maskers club to dress in a peasant skirt and boots and kerchief and help open and close Tevye's little thatched trollhouse, wheel Motel's sewing machine on and off, and so on. Also, at the end they had me carry a baby across the stage and wave sadly to Golde as we fled the pogrom. So I was one of the women of Anatevka after all, though my name wasn't on the cast list.

* * *

Brent had the biggest head I had ever seen, and he wasn't a big person, my height maybe. He was Valerie's brother, but he didn't

ANNE SHARP

look anything like her. He had mousy brown hair, long and wispy, parted on the side and brushed back from his big forehead, and slanting gray eyes. He was seven years older than Valerie and me. When I met him he was wearing a turn-of-the-century Russian student's cap and a purple blouse with gray and pink trim round the collar and down the front, and mouse-colored knickers and black boots, and he had on eyeliner and putty-colored makeup. I still remember the damp, sharp, clayey smell of that makeup, and the waxwork texture of his painted cheek. He was Fyedka, the Christian Ukrainian boy who takes away Tevye's little bird, his little Chavaleh.

I had almost met this phantom brother of Valerie's several times, but kept just missing him. I'm not sure whether he was living at home or just visited and slept there occasionally. Valerie said the only time she usually got to see him was around dinner time, when he woke up.

He gave me a ride home in his VW beetle, sooty with cigarette ash. Valerie sat in front with him; I rode in the back, with several copies of *New Music Express*, pop cans, boxes of audio cassettes, and a gray Borsalino hat.

"This is definitely the worst show I've ever been in," said Brent.

I ventured that this was the worst production of *Fiddler* I'd ever seen.

"Really? You've seen it how many times?"

"She's Jewish," said Valerie. Brent looked very interested.

I explained that I wasn't really, only half, but I had seen the show five times: 1) Madison High School, when my sister was in it (a definitive Frumah Sarah), 2) the Jewish Community Center in Oak Park, which dad took me to, 3) the movie, and 4) the Fisher Theatre in Detroit with Zero Mostel, which made the Lads production Brent and I were in 5). Actually, the Fisher was probably the worst of all. Zero Mostel had played the role of Tevye eighty zillion times by then, and chanted all the lines as though he was so bored with them we should all be ashamed of ourselves for making him say them again. From where I sat in the second balcony he had just looked like a big obnoxious brown caterpillar.

When I told Yvonne we were doing *Fiddler*, her reaction was, "Another one?!"

She couldn't believe we did a musical every year at Lads. "What do they *do*?"

I wasn't sure what she meant.

"Last year it was *The Boy Friend*, right? What did they do the year before?"

"*Little Mary Sunshine*."

"Ahhh hahhh," said Yvonne.

It seemed that last year, at the time of my *Boy Friend* audition, Yvonne had gotten into a discussion about it with some friends who were musical comedy nuts, and they had decided that it was a logical fallacy for a Catholic all-girl's school to do a yearly production of a Broadway musical the way normal high schools did. The fact that we had to import males for our productions (and Brent was actually one of our better catches, even though he could neither sing nor dance) was barely the half of it. They reasoned that with the exception of *The Boy Friend* and *Little Mary Sunshine* there wasn't anything in the Anglo-American musical theater canon that was performable at a place like Lads. They hadn't forgotten *Fiddler*, they'd just guessed wrong on it; they'd supposed a show about the persecution of Slavic Jews would be too close for comfort for Polish Christians. They'd ruled out *The Sound of Music* on similar grounds. "Anyway, they'd never let you dress up like nuns," said Yvonne.

"You don't think so?"

"We came up with a list. I'll try to remember. Okay, you can't do *Cabaret*. Can't do *Gypsy*, can't do *Hair*, can't do *Damn Yankees*, *Pajama Game*, *Mame*, *Guys and Dolls*—"

"Why not *Mame*?"

"Agnes Gooch," said Yvonne.

Quite right. No unwed mothers at Lads—it would be straight to Sinai for Agnes.

"Can't do *Kismet*," Yvonne was saying. "Can't do *Music Man*."

"Why not?"

"It's too dirty. Let's see, you definitely couldn't do *She Loves Me*."

"What's that?"

"It's this really cute show about Hungarians in a drug store; it's too dirty. I don't know about *Annie Get Your Gun*; I guess you could make some cuts and clean it up a little but what's the point. You couldn't do *West Side Story*, but nobody can do that at a high school because Leonard Bernstein makes you do it with a full orchestra. It has people screwing in it anyway. You can't do *How to Succeed in Business*, can't do *Pal Joey*, can't do *Funny Thing Happened on the Way to the Forum*, can't do *Camelot*, can't do *Man of La Mancha*, can't do *Funny Girl* . . . well, you wouldn't want to do *Funny Girl*, it sucks. I *guess* you could do *Hello, Dolly*, though it doesn't have that many good women's roles, really. You can forget about *My Fair Lady*."

"Why?"

"There's only one decent part for a woman in it, and I doubt they could come up with a Henry Higgins if they can't even find a good Tevye." (Yeah.) "I mean, all the best shows in the repertoire. Why do they try?"

"Couldn't they do Rodgers and Hammerstein?"

"Look," said Yvonne. "You've got *Oklahoma*. That's got pornography, murder, people fucking in haystacks. *Carousel*'s got murder, crime, fornication. *South Pacific*'s got interracial sex and that guy with the cocoanut tits. *The King and I* has too many little kids in it, that's better for community theater. Look, Rodgers and Hammerstein is the least likely. It's pure sex and violence, and you know what else, it's radical. It's anti-racist, anti-dictator. Those people at your school have to watch their asses, if they get out of line the Pope pulls their license. What do you bet they get complaints about doing *Fiddler*? People who don't want their kids doing a Jewish play? I think you're just going to be doing *Little Mary Sunshine* and *The Boy Friend* in rotation for a while after this."

*   *   *

Brent told me he had friends who worked for the Ann Arbor film societies, and that if I had any movies I really wanted to see he could suggest them to them. At first I thought I should be unselfish and ask Neil and Dave what they wanted to see. Then I thought I should ask for the things I thought I ought to see, like *The Passion of Joan of Arc* and *El Topo.*

Then one morning in class I just wrote down my true top ten, which was:

1. *Der Verlorene* ("The Lost One")
2. *Mad Love*
3. *Crime and Punishment*
4. *I Was An Adventuress*
5. *The Constant Nymph*
6. *Background to Danger*
7. *Stranger on the Third Floor*
8. *Strange Cargo*
9. *The Boogie Man Will Get You*
10. *You'll Find Out*

Brent took my list after that night's performance with a gracious smile. "If they show one of these," he said, "can I go with you?"

Could he go with me. How else would I get there? I still couldn't drive. And I realized then that he really had to take me, because I wouldn't want to see any of these with Neil and Dave. Not *Mad Love,* anyway.

*   *   *

It was in the spring of my senior year that I first started hearing about Natalie's fiancé. I had lost track of the details of her life by then, my own life having become comparatively eventful, so this new state of affairs came as a big surprise. I don't know where they found this guy. He was a sweet, soft, shambling young man in polyester pants who had a very good job at one of the Big Three, and he thought Natalie was an angel off the top of the tree. Natalie herself seemed to think it was all just fine. She met his parents, and they liked her. Everybody was Catholic, so there was no problem there.

Natalie's mother was taking no chances. Despite the short lead time, immediately after Natalie got the ring she made arrangements for a full-scale wedding to take place in late summer. I was still Natalie's official dearest friend, and though I wasn't in on the planning (they might as well have asked the white poodle to help, as she probably knew more about weddings than I did) I was going to be in the wedding party. Not as maid of honor; that was dearest, not best, remember. That position went to Joy, who was to wear electric pink. Peggy and Denise and I were to be the rank-and-file bridesmaids in electric blue.

Peggy took me with her to Kitty Kelly's for our fittings. Those dresses were heavy duty late seventies polyester, like wearing vinyl siding, but they were theatrical costumes after all; the main thing was they wouldn't wrinkle. I was pleased by the somewhat early thirties cut of the gown, and by the fact that at Kitty's I magically became a size 8, for the first and only time in my life.

Driving me home from our initial encounter with our new synthetic casings, Peggy lit a Kent and offered me one. "This is such a joke," she said.

I was startled, but since she came out with it with such candor I agreed it would never last, that she would probably run off with the milkman by the end of the year.

"Still," said Peggy, with a suck of Kent, "if it makes her happy, why not, shit. It should be a good party. You ever been to a Polish wedding?"

No, I said.

"*Oooooaahh*," said Peggy, exhaling keenly through her teeth. "*Noooobody* parties like the Polacks."

* * *

I would graduate soon and be an adult; now I really had to get a driver's license. I could probably arrange a life in which operating a motor vehicle was never necessary, but what about cashing checks and buying liquor? So I enrolled in a commercial driving school. They had a special interest in passing you at these places that the smug smedleys teaching public school driver's ed didn't, so they didn't fleer at you if you didn't know which stick was the shift; they just told you. They only showed one upsetting film to us, and even this one they allowed us to skip, athough our classroom instructor was pleased to give us a verbal preview. The film featured footage of real car accidents. "Yeah, you'll be amazed," he said with relish. "Especially when you see that one lady who has her thigh bones comin' up out of her shoulders . . . yeah, it's quite a sight. . . ."

There was one day I came close to losing my nerve. The car from the driving school that came to pick me up was not my usual car, driven by a gentle fatherly teacher with an Appalachian twang. This was a man I'd never seen before, a little whiny guy of the sort my sister and her friends used to call a Poindexter.

He was sulky with us at first, but perked up when we picked up one of the other students, a pretty and pleasant girl with fluffy reddish hair and a chain with two transposed golden triangles dangling on her collarbone. "You're also Jewish?" he asked, his voice rising an octave.

"Yeah."

"You must feel cut off from the whole Jewish world, living out here."

I said, "There are Jews in Prague. I'm half Jewish."

The guy turned to me and gave me a look as though I was something he wanted to scrape immediately off the bottom of his shoe.

I said no more until it was my turn behind the wheel. He steered me towards that stretch of I-275 near my mom's house that always reminded me of a slot car race, and down the entrance ramp. "Now remember," he said, as I did this, "there are only two kinds of people on the freeway, the quick and the dead."

As I merged, my blood started to fizz. A wholly new form of existential horror possessed me as I forced myself down this concrete gauntlet with two tons of metal death six inches away on either side of me, and gaining on me from behind. "Keep telling yourself," said Mr. Racial Purity, "it's only a movie."

I graduated from that driver's school. I got my license. I never set a tire on the freeway again.

* * *

They say that it takes you several tries to actually feel anything when you first start smoking marijuana. Well, I had thought I'd gotten high right away the first time. It was back when Yvonne was still a teeny-bopper, and we had spent the day traipsing around Ann Arbor poking through all the head shops and Indian cotton clothing boutiques. We must have looked conspicuously like little suburban girls, because an old hippie guy befriended us in the Diag, sat us down in the grass next to Angell Hall, and gave us pot to smoke.

He took an unfiltered Camel and manipulated it so the tobacco in the lower end loosened and could be shaken out. Then he took out a self-sealing sandwich bag (for years the only self-sealing bags I ever saw were dope bags—the drug trade was a real change leader with this product) and packed the empty space in the paper tube with weed. Then he lit it and passed it among us three. I remember everything being very still and soft-focus, and then wandering off by myself to Burger King to order the most wonderful Dr Pepper of my life.

"You can't have been high," Yvonne said later, and maybe she was right. I am highly suggestible.

I smoked from then on without incident, happily unaffected. I bought a nickel bag from Natalie once—dealing was a very casual line of hers for a while—and every so often after mom left in the mornings I would go out on the patio for a puff before school.

What happened to all that dope in that bag? There was tons of it, I couldn't possibly have smoked it all myself. But it wasn't very good, I remember; maybe I threw it out or gave it away. It was definitely not that pot, the only stuff I ever bought, that I smoked in the woods with Neil that spring. Where he got it, I don't know.

We had gone off for a walk near his house, and were in the wood behind the elementary school where he used to go. We had my pipe, a little beauty with a silver bowl and mouthpiece and a green glass stem you could see the smoke going through before it got too dirty. As I remember it, I had only taken a pull or two at the pipe when the world altered itself.

The horizon became a sort of pillow shape, wide in dead center and pinched at both ends of my peripheral vision. I moved in a world that bulged at the top and narrowed away to nothing at the sides, no matter where I looked, which made me turn faster and faster, panicked, hoping to find where this twisted perspective stopped. Everything was very bright and the colors were piercing. My voice, and Neil's, sounded tinny and muffled. I couldn't remember my name or where I was. I realized that I must be insane, and the thought that my brain would be like this for the rest of my life was unbearably terrifying. I scampered and stumbled. "Bobby," I said, "Bobby, take me to the hospital." Neil was Bobby, I don't know why.

"Okay."

"Take me to the hospital!"

"O-okay."

We traded this frantic call-and-response, me pacing around and Neil trying to follow me without making any startling moves, until I became less agitated and more petrified. He walked me over to a nearby party store and had me sit on one of the parking lot curb markers while he went in. I sat there stunned, afraid to move, until he came out with a box of doughnuts and had me eat them. I ate, thinking, I'll be like this forever.

But Neil's doughnut remedy worked, because by the time he got me back to his house and put me on the couch in his basement I didn't feel frightened anymore. I was just sad, thinking about how I'd lost my mind, not noticing it was already back.

Later Neil said he thought the pot must have had angel dust in it. But no, as it turned out that was just what marijuana did to me. It wrapped a muffle around the parts of my brain that reasoned, and left me like a pithed reptile, all quivering instinct without a pilot there. That Dr Pepper day in the Diag was the only pleasant high I would ever have in my life off of this particular substance. Liquor I could tolerate, because although it took away my reason, it also shut down the parts that cared. But the dread of what had happened in those woods made me never want to sample cocaine, LSD, amphetamines, even helium, or any of the other things people around me have used to color their minds like Easter eggs. What's a reliable source of fun to them is potential Horror City to me. The worst thing about consciousness-altering drugs is that once you take them, they won't stop until they're through with you, whatever that means and however long it takes. No. I've had enough other things like that in my life.

* * *

That is all I remember from my last months in high school: fear. Just shivering waves of sweat, with my exhausted heart pounding, and the world shimmering around me in grainy half-focus. Maybe everybody feels this way as they approach graduation, the official death of childhood. It felt to me exactly the way it feels when you first realize as a child that you are actually, personally, going to die someday. Only what's frightening now is life—always a scarier proposition than death.

I had never lived so continuously in such absolute terror. It never went away. I could be taking a shower, or watching a funny movie, or eating ice cream with friends. There it was, banging on my head, this big gray skull thing. Even crying didn't relieve it. Alcohol made it worse. I became a temporary abstainer. But nothing made it stop.

In the midst of this, the senior class took its traditional year-end trip to Cedar Point, to ride the scary rides. I wasn't particularly interested in going on the Blue Streak or the Wild Mouse. I went basically for the chance to smoke and to be with all my friends from school, most of whom I never intended to see again once I got out. I just wanted to go with them to the waving-off point, as they went on to whatever toy-scattered suburban living room, trailer park or brothel lay in their futures.

We went in a pack, Ruthie and me and the girls, in the back of the same bus. Some of us were missing. Valerie didn't go, and I didn't see Natalie either; if she'd wanted to go to Cedar Point, she probably would have gone with her fiancé.

When you hear about something that frightens you as a child, there is always a special frisson when you finally see it, no matter what age you are. The Ghost Town in Frontierland didn't disappoint me at all. That was the part I always made my friends tell me about when I was a little kid, and I was so glad when Ruthie and the others got right on the train that took you there, right after we got to the park.

How utterly satisfactory in presentation, this little mock-up Wild West town among the weeds, with joined skeletons in cowboy hats and barroom flounces lounging on its porches. Imagine if you fell off the train and got stranded there at night. Or even in the daytime. What if they came alive, these skeletons? and what if they didn't? How terrible their stillness would be.

At this time, there still weren't any truly horrific rides at Cedar Point; nothing that whipped you around in pitch blackness or dropped you ten stories at g-force velocity. We went on the race horses, the antique cars, the bumper cars, the wavy thing that goes around like a bobsled, the octopus thing, the cable car. That last one was a bit of a butt-tightener, especially when the other girls wriggled around and made it rock on its cable, the tensile strength of which I had absolutely no faith in. But nothing scared me. We went on the Mine Ride, a minor wooden semicoaster that shook a lot; it vibrated the glasses right off my nose. We looked for them in the weeds underneath the ride afterwards, but those glasses were lost forever. So the rest of the day was an ethereal blur to me.

I couldn't see distances, but I could make out what was immediately there. So when we went into the little aquarium, a damp dark concrete hall like a sideshow version of the Belle Isle fish caverns, I could see clearly the tank of moray eels standing on end with their tails hidden in the rocks and their necks craned like soft brown candy canes, eyes and mouths gaping wide in an unsettlingly chummy grin. And when I went on the Blue Streak, I ratcheted up unknowable distances into the air, then plunged into unforeseeable nothingnesses. I couldn't imagine how anyone could find this enjoyable: it was basically a machine for duplicating the sensation you have in dreams in which you are plummeting to your death. Well, there is no disputing tastes.

So this, at last, was Cedar Point, what I'd waited seventeen years to see. I left its macabre attractions at the end of the day without regret. I'd done it, and at the appropriate time, while I was still young, and now I never had to do it again. Next item, a new pair of glasses.

"Why don't you get contacts?" Yvonne asked. "They're a lot better for your eyes. Your prescription doesn't change as much."

Now here was a phobia I hadn't even known I had. It had been hard for me to use eye drops, and when I went to the optometrist it was all I could do to keep my eyes open when I tried to stare at the little dot of light that allowed him to glimpse the veins in my eyeball. Now, sitting in the examination chair, it dawned on me that not only was I going to have to learn to touch the surface of my own eye, but that this optometrist expected me to allow him to put a test set of lenses in my eyes, apparently intending to use a pair of enormous plastic tongs to do this.

"I'm sorry, no," I said, leaping out of the chair.

But Yvonne made me go back. I got through the eyeball fittings, and then, when my new contacts came in, went back to take the little class with the optical assistant (or whatever they call them, those women in nurse white that are the equivalent of dental assistants in optical shops) that they make you go through before you can take the lenses home.

I did everything the optical assistant told us to do, but though the rest of the group caught on quickly, I still couldn't get my fingertip to touch my eye steadily enough so that the little plastic saucer on the end of it could click onto my iris. The optical assistant actually would not let me have my contacts. She made me come back in a week for another class. This was drivers' ed all over again.

I really tried hard, though. The natural desensitization process helped, and during that second session I got them in, right on target, first try. The optical assistant was satisfied and let me have them.

Now I could see everything, out of the corners of my eyes, down my cheeks, up towards my forehead, every vista unimpeded. And for the first time since I had gotten my first pair of glasses at age seven, other people could see my eyes, not reduced in size by concave lenses but in their actual proportions and dimensions. I couldn't tell you objectively what difference this made in my life. But you know what always happens in the movies.

*   *   *

I wished I could have just ignored my high school graduation instead of having to go to it, but I wasn't flamboyant enough. I wore my green mortarboard and took my blank scroll from Sr. Magda and the kiss from my relieved mother, just like a normal girl. But I did skip all the parties that night. The most egregious skip was Valerie's party, because not only did I snub her, I stole her brother. Brent and Neil came over for dinner, and then the three of us went to Ann Arbor to see *Aguirre, the Wrath of God.*

All my terror and pity that night were drawn up into the ruined, feral face of Klaus Kinski, spread monumentally over the screening wall of Aud. A, Angell Hall. That final scene on the Amazon River: talk about an objective correlative that just won't quit. Was I the monkey that night, having the shit shaken out of me on that spinning raft by that terrifying Pole, or was I the crazed shaker?

That was it for my life as a Catholic high school girl. I sold my skirt to a sophomore, and the saddle shoes went into the basement. They and the glow-in-the-dark Fatima rosary were all I had to prove I had ever been there. That and the yearbooks. But I hadn't bought the last one, and I had purposefully neglected to pose for my senior picture. If you look in the Lads yearbook for 1976-77, over my name you'll see a gray square of half-tone. Remember me when this you see.

7. ALL THROUGH THE NIGHT

Brent and I were the only people in Aud. A that night. the night we went alone. Up until they lowered the lights, it looked as though we would have a private screening. But as they showed the previews for the film coop's next show, *Shadows of Forgotten Ancestors*, a pack of young men in frowzy T-shirts came in and sat directly behind us. I heard a match sizzle, and presently a crepuscular aura of dope smoke softened our view of the screen.

Title sequence: an orchestral crescendo. A window, edged with frost, overlooking some dark wintry scene. The squat shadow of a man falls over the sill.

The camera glances frantically now at what seems to be a series of adjoining windows, each set of frozen panes revealing a different vista of Paris rooftops at night. cathedral spires, gargoyles. Someone has breathed over one of the panes, and written "Mad Love" in the mist with his finger. At the last window, a little fist bobs up and punches through the pane.

And so I was initiated into the strange and beguiling romance of Professor Gogol. Napoleon of orthopedic medicine, holy infant in furs, courtly lover of somber music and English poetry. masturbator in Parisian snuff shows, with his wild extremes of noble and contemptible behavior, in his attempts to obtain a woman he hasn't got the least idea what to do with. I loved it better than a thousand *Rocky Horrors*. I bathed in its rococo perversities; I gave no thought to its unsettling implications, this story of a lonely soul brought down by his insensate passion for an unpossessable creature of the theater. It was beauty killed the beast; ohhh, isn't it always?

They didn't have a roll of credits for films of this period. After "The End," they just flashed a page of principal players and the NRA symbol ("We Do Our Part.") I didn't feel the usual pull to leave after the lights went on again. I went forward and stepped onto the stage. With no one stopping me, I touched the beaded screen where he had been.

Brent led me out across the quad. There was a big white moon up there. "I'm almost afraid to look at it, like it would have his face," said Brent. "Poor little P.L."

That beautiful white face of a crafty Buddha; it had glowed. Papa Freund had made it up and lit it like the face of the moon. You could tell in the scene where he was supposed to kiss Frances Drake that they were both careful to do it so their thickly stylized makeups didn't touch.

He took me to a place he called Thanatos' Lamplighter, and ordered me pizza and pop, and allowed me to dabble in his pack of unfiltered Camels, which knocked the breath out of me. Then he asked if I had to go home yet; he hoped not, because he wanted to show me his radio station.

He led me down the street, past the huge black cube standing on point that you could spin like a top, to a hideous glass-and-steel old building, to the basement of this building, through a bare ugly entryway into a half-lit maze of glassed-in cubicles. These were the radio studios. He showed me one tiny glass cube with a guy in it, turntable in front of him like a dinner plate, a microphone hanging in front of his lips. "That's the AM station," Brent said, a little pityingly.

The FM station, Brent's station, was spread over several rooms. Brent took me around, introducing me to the people we met as "my friend." He showed me the studio where he did his own show—not tonight, though—the turntables, the cartridge decks, the ashtrays and hand puppets and empty pint bottles. The show currently in progress was next door; some older guy with a ponytail was the deejay. He waved his cigarette at us. We waited until he'd stopped talking, then went in. "Taking any requests tonight?" asked Brent.

"Well, what would the *lady* like to hear?"

I looked at the shelves. It was a classic jazz show; let's see. Wasn't there something I'd always wanted to hear, that Jim Gallert had never played? Oh, *yeah*. And here it was. What a night.

I gave it to the guy with the ponytail. "Ahh, the Hungarian Suicide Song!" he chortled, slipping it out of its sleeve without touching the black part, sliding it onto the spindle. We sat together as those minatory saxophones spoke in hushed tones over the speakers above us, as Billie Holiday stoically intoned the words, "Sunday is gloomy. . . ."

"I got the tape back," said the ponytail man suddenly, during the instrumental bridge.

Brent's narrow eyes suddenly shone. "Can you make me a copy?" he whispered.

The man nodded, held up his finger.

They listened, not moving, as the song meandered to its funereal close. "You are the darkest woman I know," said Brent, putting the record back in its sleeve with a staring smile.

"Anyway," said the man. "It's not as good as the first one. DAMN I wish we had that one."

"Oh, it's heartbreaking," said Brent.

It seemed that last December, the ponytail man had decided to play all nine of Beethoven's symphonies simultaneously, in honor of his birthday. But something had gone wrong, and the engineer had failed to record it for posterity. A recent attempt to recreate the broadcast just hadn't hit the mark; this was the one that he was going to make a copy of for Brent. What had it been like, the real thing, I asked.

"Like," said the ponytail man, forgetting his ashefying cigarette on the edge of a stack of LPs, "this wall of sound. . . . It was like, sometimes they'd all fit perfectly, they'd all be in harmony, or sometimes they'd all just stop at the same time. The Ninth lasted the longest. It was. . . . yeah, it was intense. Calls started coming in, there must have been about seventy people called while it was happening. This one old lady said, 'I think you're playing two things at the same time!' One guy got really irate, he said he couldn't hear the

Second, he thought we'd left it out. And then these two cops showed up. Somebody called them, they came to see if there was anyone still alive in the station. . . ."

Brent smiled as we walked to the car. He wasn't looking at me. I felt as though he'd forgotten I was there, until he ran around to open the car door for me. Brent smiled a lot, I realized, not because of anything particular that was happening to him at the time, but at the prompting of some inner stimulus, beyond the normal planes of perception.

After we got in the car, he took a tape out of his pocket, punched it into the dashboard tape deck, tossed the plastic case into the ash-spattered recess next to the stick shift and smiled his quiet smile, this time looking straight at me.

It was the Spike Jones version of "My Old Flame," with the vocal by Paul Frees, doing an impression of . . . you know. You've probably heard it. "I can't even think of her name—I'll have to look through my collection of human heads." I'd heard this thing many times before, on Dr. Demento, on the Sir Graves show, and had no desire to hear it again. But I suffered myself to listen, for Brent had made an offering of it to me, and that kindness of intention neutralized its obscenity somewhat, made it even worthy of hearing out somehow.

This slavering collector of human heads, this gibbering setter-on-fire of women: was this my Gogol, my deity of purest alabaster? *Spike Jones* thought so; *Paul Frees* thought so; *Brent* even thought so. Doting girl that I was, though, I refused to see it.

When we pulled up in my driveway, it was midnight. Brent turned and looked at me, again with that smile, not saying anything for longer than was socially comfortable.

"Goodnight," he said finally.

"Don't forget your tape," he said, as I scrambled out of the beetle. I took it from his chilly hand. As I went in, I noticed him still in the driveway, not moving, smiling at—what.

* * *

Brent told me the call letters and dial number of his station, but warned me it wasn't easy to tune in all the way out in Prague, twenty-five miles east of Ann Arbor; being a student station, it didn't broadcast at very high power. I couldn't get it on my clock radio, but sometimes late at night I could pick it up on the Magnavox console in the living room. Brent's show was on from two to four AM, Monday through Thursday. It was called *Greetings, Earthlings*, and at that time of the morning it was very easy to disbelieve what you were hearing, to imagine you'd dozed off and dreamed what you'd been listening to, which made it seem even stranger.

It was on this show that I heard punk for the very first time, or rather what was more properly known then as New Wave, the British Invasion bands of the late 70s. Brent also played a lot of New Wave allies and forerunners: the Stooges, MC5, the Velvet Underground together and in its component parts, Roxy Music, the Tubes. But the real rhythm of the show, especially as it stretched into its second hour, was less pop music-oriented, more in the nature of a wayward hallucination. There were uncredited snatches of Firesign Theatre and Caedmon literature recordings, long passages from Crumb, Varese and *Metal Machine Music*, and occasional orphic monologues by Brent himself. It's those dead-of-night soundscapes that I most closely associate with my memories of Brent, distant, shifting, brilliant and vague, in heart-rending minor keys.

* * *

It happened that the morning after my mom threw my dad out of the house was the morning they gave my sister's seventh grade class the PSAT, the standardized test that decides a child's future worth to society. Because of this monstrous trick of timing, for the rest of her school life Yvonne's teachers, counselors, principals, and mother wondered how this girl could be so well spoken and do so well in all her classes while participating in so many extracurricular activities, given her subnormal intelligence rating. They decided she was an overachiever, and got more and more impatient at her persistence in behaving like an extremely bright young woman, excelling at so many things she wasn't supposed to be able to do (like acing her SATs). Getting a free ride to one of the top private colleges in the country was the final straw; I thought they were going to storm the house with torches and farm implements.

I, on the other hand, lay around like a lox all through my developmental years, but my school records all had me pegged in the gifted category, since I had done wonderfully on my PSAT, as I did on all standardized tests. Being neurasthenic and dazed with lack of sleep, caring nothing for my future, it didn't matter to me how I scored. I was totally relaxed going into those tests, which gave me a tremendous advantage over all those conscientious students fumbling and going dry from fear.

It was my SAT score, surely not my grade point (2.9) or extracurricular activities (smoking, putting on eyeliner, watching movies and writing long passionate diary entries on them) that got me into the University of Michigan. I'm not even sure why I applied there, except that it was the local college and I liked Ann Arbor. Anyway, they said they'd take me and for the next few months I obligingly filled out the packets of forms they kept sending me, not really taking it seriously, not comprehending that the thrust of all this would be that at the end of the summer I would leave my mother's house and my life would change quite dramatically.

Under the terms of my state academic grant, I had to have a summer job to earn money towards my college expenses, so I went to work as a waitress at the Big Boy near my house. I wasn't very good at it, so they usually sent me home early if they weren't busy. That meant I had most of my evenings free to visit Neil's basement.

"What would you do if there weren't any movies?" I asked Neil one time.

"Oh, I'd do something else," he replied. I was amazed at his confidence in this.

One weekend in July I was supposed to go out to Ann Arbor for my orientation at the university. My mother offered to take me, but I said no thank you. I was already going with Neil and Dave.

We got there early, had lunch at Krazy Jim's, and then they dropped me off and went to go paw through the used record stores for soundtracks. Both were sullen and hadn't had much to say to me. Though I tried to tell them it would be just as good as before, that we'd still go to the film coops together and everything, they knew better and treated me like the traitor I was, going off to school without them.

The first thing the orientation leaders did with us was to take us over to the athletic building near the stadium, where they had us lie on our backs and kick one of those big bladder balls around. Oh my GOD I thought, my primal fear of gym coming over me. But it was a false alarm, just a group bonding exercise. It would be the last coercive physical activity I would ever experience for the rest of my (academic) life.

I would never have to take math again, either. The worst I would have to do was to put up with one more science course, to fulfill my distribution requirements. I chose physical anthropology, the study of ape men. And Intro to Psych, and Intro to Journalism, and Intro to Film, and Great Books (another requirement). The counselor stamped my course sheet, and then our orientation leaders trooped us all over to CRISP (located in Angell Hall) to register us for our classes and issue us our blue-and-gold student identity cards.

They were so solicitous of us, concerned that we not be frightened by the big university and feel driven to jump off the top of the bell tower (as several students would do later that semester). They took us to the libraries we would be using, the Gradli and the Ugli, and to the Central Campus Recreation Building, where were invited to visit anytime, to run and swim and swat off our academically-induced panic attacks. To further relax us, they gave us a party in the dorm where we were staying, featuring actual kegs of beer.

My dorm mate that weekend was Jennifer Cislo from Grosse Pointe. She was gracious and pretty and vivacious, and had been valedictorian of her class. We liked each other a lot and by the night of the kegger were discussing changing my dorm assignment so I could room with her that fall. (She was going to be in Mary Markley, which was supposed to be one of the nicest dorms, but I had been booked into South Quad, which everyone at orientation said sucked.)

Maybe it was the dull not-so-heavy metal music, or the unspeakable freshman guys panting with naked visions of *Penthouse*'s "Girls of the Big Ten" in their eyes, or the hideous children's hospital playroom they called the study lounge where the party took place, but Jennifer and I fled the kegger and ended up two floors below in the darkened dining hall, dancing on the tables. I starting singing selections from *Valmouth* (which Yvonne had thoughtfully put on the other side of my *Boy Friend* tape.) Jennifer set down her cup of beer and fell like a petal onto one of the cafeteria benches.

"Just think," she murmured. "Some day everyone in this building will be dead.'

A couple of months after this, around midterms, Jennifer called me in a disoriented, nervous state; she saw bats flying around her dorm room. At least they weren't telling her to jump off the bell tower. I tried to reassure her that it was all right, that she should just lie down and listen to some George Benson, and when she felt better go talk to her residence hall adviser. Apparently this worked and they managed to calm her and send her home, where she made a successful recovery. I am sorry I couldn't have been there to comfort her and ease her through her confrontation with the Great God Pan, whom I've met many times myself. But other plans had been made for me.

*   *   *

In my childhood summers, vacations had meant going to concerts and museums and plays with my culture vulture parents. Now, at seventeen, I was finally getting taken to the childish play places my friends were by this time blase about. First Cedar Point, now Boblo. Could Disneyland be that far down the line?

I went with Yvonne and some of her friends for an evening cruise to Boblo. The riverboat was great; they had a band of little old guys in straw hats playing oompah music, a bar, and lots of places to lounge on the deck and smoke. When we got to the island itself, I went on the mechanical swings with Yvonne, but didn't feel like trying any of the other rides. So while she and her friends ran around, I went to the pavilion, scored a boxful of those wonderful lung-rasping Canadian cigarettes (what drugs they were! two puffs and you were dizzy as a dervish), and sat around eavesdropping, which I'd recently realized was one of my life's callings.

They didn't give you much time on the island. Before I even had time to bore myself it was time to get back on the boat. Yvonne and I pounced up the gangplank, then from the railing serenaded our island friends with our by now perfected rendition of "You Could Drive a Person Crazy." We were such a couple of showboats.

We had a great time on the trip back. I must have seemed like such a fun girl, I was asked to dance. This guy was a few years older than me, taller and much thinner than me, with opalescent skin and blue-black hair and a bony-cheekboned face, pale gray-green eyes, a long slender nose with a little cleft, and scarlet lips parted over teeth in an effect reminiscent of Klaus Kinski in *Nosferatu*. Really, he was quite handsome.

We danced to the silly old music, with his hands on my waist, mine on his shoulders. Not real couple dancing, a nearly extinct discipline by the time my generation came along, but I improvised under his guidance, and it seemed to fit. He was quiet and wry and surprisingly interested in me. Before we disembarked in Detroit again, he had taken me off to a dark part of the deck to make out.

Yvonne was bemused. "Nobody's going to lead you astray," she told me on the way home. "You're going to know where you're going and go exactly where you want to go."

We had exchanged names and phone numbers. His name was Mark Ferenzy. Oh, yes. I had had no idea there were Hungarians in Detroit, but there was apparently quite a nest of them in a place called Del Rey.

He took me on my first authentic date. We went to the Terrace to see *Star Wars*. (I'd already seen it twice, but that didn't matter. Every time I see that movie, no matter how many times it's been, I always find myself saying to myself "I don't remember this part" all the way through it.)

After *Star Wars* we went to a place across the street where we had some cheesecake that we both disapproved of. "What do you want to do now?" he asked. I didn't know, so he took me to Detroit to see his brother.

Mark's brother was very amusing, a gruff Furry Freak Brothers type. He seemed glad we'd stopped by, as he wanted to show off his newest possessions: some lighting fixtures that had been stripped off one of the old downtown movie palaces that had gone to seed and kung fu movies before closing down. I'd never been in any of those theaters, the Fox or the State or the Grand Circus. Out of context, these wildly ornamented Art Deco teratomas looked to me like something from the movies themselves, props from a Garbo picture that had fallen from the heavens into this little bewildered house in Del Rey.

Mark's brother treated us to some hilarious muttered rants, mostly about his cat Doofus, who seemed like a sweet, ordinary pink tabby to me, but whom this man seemed to think was contemptibly dumb. He told us Doofus anecdotes: how Doofus ate all the leftover peas at Thanksgiving, how he put Doofus in a paper bag once and puffed dope smoke at him. How *angry* he was at Doofus. And how unconcerned Doofus was at his master's display of indignation: casually curling around our legs, sniffing the scent of my dog on my ankles and then with understated bravado marking me with his whiskers.

We went back to my house. It was 2 AM by then, and my mother was asleep. There was a big soft red plush sectional in the living room, and it was there that this patient and generous man introduced me to the pleasures of men.

I don't mean the penis. That would come soon enough. This, now, was enjoyment of a familiar kind, but done in a new way. Sensible man. You start a woman off with what she's used to. So I felt no fear, no pain, and there was no danger to my white shorts; just boundless affection and gratitude on my part. He could have gone further. I would have stayed wound around him all night, whatever he'd done, he made me so happy. But he was that rare sort of soul, a social sexual being, who could sense when things had gone far enough. So he rocked himself loose from me and went home at around 5 AM. I went to bed but there are states of physical arousal that override sleep, and I'd had enough of just staying up late; I was ready to go on till morning.

* * *

Being who and what I was, I was so far beyond the realm of normal dating that if you had asked me at any time during my high school days when the prom was, I honestly couldn't have told you. But as Labor Day crept nearer, my lack of suitors suddenly became a problem. I had to find a man to go with me to Natalie's wedding. The role of escort to this fertility rite needed to be cast with care. Neil would be shy and contemptuous, and want to go home to watch Elwy. Taking Brent would be like going with a helium balloon. The obvious choice for fun and maximum presentability was my new friend Hungarian Mark. I called him and he said yes.

He arrived in a cue-chalk-blue leisure suit, which coordinated perfectly with my Kitty Kelly bridesmaid's gown. The rest of the evening was just full of such harmonies. He knew all the stuff to do in church, being Catholic, so he wasn't bored sitting alone waiting for me while I was up there during the ceremony. He was actually quite popular with the ushers, I learned later, because he had brought joints. He was very patient and good at posing for all the pictures; he liked the food; he knew the best things to order at the VFW hall bar; he was sweet and made jokes with all the old people; he danced with me to everything, including the polkas; in short, was a perfect Eastern European gentleman.

I'm afraid we behaved disgustingly. We made out right at the bridal table. They *loved* it. Peggy was right about Polish wedding receptions. The old people had just started getting really smashed, and steam was rising off the polka floor by the time we gave up and stumbled out.

He stopped by a party store on Joy Road and got a six pack of Labatts, drove me to Hines Park, took me up on one of the ridges, and I will never forgive the policeman who interrupted and made us go home. This should been my first man.

* * *

It wasn't until I read Neal Gabler's *An Empire of Their Own* that I had any idea there was a hierarchy of Jews. But just as the African American community had its paper bag test, the Jewish American world in the early twentieth century had its method of ranking itself, by geographical origin. At the top were the German Jews. Then the Eastern Europeans, and then down at the bottom there were my people, or rather my father's people, the Russian Jews.

The men who made and managed the Hollywood studios were determined to be as American, or at least as German, as possible. That meant following an Anglo-Saxon ideal of high culture and Republican notions of what constituted class. They kept their visible Judaism to a minimum, permitting Christian pressure groups to censor and dictate the contents of their pictures, and hiring the whitest-looking talent they could find to put in front of the cameras. You could make Louis B. Mayer cry by singing "My Yiddishe Momma," but give him a snub-nosed goy like Greer Garson for the ultimate screen madonna. For these men, the Hollywood ideal of passing was Leslie Howard, so radiantly English as the dimpled blond Southern Adonis Ashley Wilkes that you'd never know his parents were Hungarians named Stainer.

They loved to have him around, I think. I mean, *him*. He was a reminder of what they were so desperately trying to leave behind, but what stuck to them, never left them, like the accent he never lost. That sound, like a howl from the wilderness of the old country, tagged him, made his origins identifiable wherever he went. He was a natural to play the stranger male the immigration reformers and eugeni-cists were so horrified of, the one you *really* wouldn't want around your women. Tucked into dozens and dozens of pictures, radio shows, television shows, he was their mascot, their shadow emissary into white-bread Middle America, half-disavowed by them, given despi-cable roles, chuckled over affectionately. Their old flame.

* * *

When I called Yvonne and told her our grandmother had died, she said, "Good!" She had been our last grandparent, our father's mother. Yvonne said she remembered how we'd go over to her mothbally old building downtown with the pimps in the lobby, and how she'd be sitting there talking about the Goyim. "Those people never gave a fuck about us," Yvonne said.

I remembered one time when I was little, my mother coming home one night from a wedding, very angry. They'd invited her and my father, but not my sister and me. But there had been other chil-dren there. *Their* children.

I got to attend one of my dad's relatives' weddings, and recall very clearly my dad in his white satin skullcap taken from a box by the door, the ceremony under the canopy, the glass wrapped in a handkerchief smashed under the heel. But we hadn't gone to the re-ception afterwards, Yvonne and I; again, we hadn't been invited, and had to be taken home to stay with a babysitter while mom went back to join dad at the party. My mother had been outraged at the little girls she'd seen that night dancing in their fluffy cute dresses, being fussed over. She brought home a white bakery box full of little cakes, with every kind of fruit, every shade of chocolate, every type of sugar known to bakers, all frilly white and silver and pastels. It was like a wedding in a box. But she couldn't bring home the band so Yvonne and I could have a dance.

Funerals are not by invitation. I went to the ceremony for my grandmother at Ira Kaufman's. You would have thought my morbid curiosity would have been prodding me to go look at her in her box, but I clung to the opposite end of the room. If I'd known her well, maybe I would have, but this wasn't the time to get close. I kept looking at dad. He'd lost his mama. I said nothing, but hugged him, which seemed to be the right thing.

Afterwards, we went to my uncle's house to sit shiva, a tradition that seemed to involve eating a lot of cake and talking about everything but the dead person. The only time I heard her mentioned there was when I was sitting on my uncle's bed, waiting for the bathroom to be unoccupied. My uncle came in with a carton of mentholated cigarettes.

"You smoke?" he asked me pleasantly. I admitted it.

"Here," he said, and gave me the carton. "These were hers."

I later showed them to my mother. "Well, that should make you quit!" she said naively.

* * *

Mom and dad were damned from the start. As very young people, they floated as depressive wisps through the forties, that appallingly cheery decade. Then the fifties came sidling up and said, okay, here's a job for you, dad, and a little house in the suburbs for mom, now breed. This was their big chance to be normal. They tried, but they couldn't, and they would never forgive each other.

This was the great exciting tragedy of their lives, this failure to make a family out of each other. And they were bound together in this hideous mutual catastrophe because they had created us children together. Still, mom had seen a way out of it: she thought, maybe rightly, that it would save all of us. It demanded so little of Yvonne and me. Just forget your father, pretend like you don't have one, is that hard? don't you get it? you'll break the spell, and we'll all be free of that horrible man forever. But I had to follow that biblical injunction, to honor both mother and father. (Is that bizarre? does a *Unitarian* have to follow the Ten Commandments?) Because of this perversity of mine, my parents were fatefully joined in eternity, like Holmes and Moriarty, locked in a deathly grapple as they went over the falls together. I tried not to look as I went away.

* * *

The night of my grandmother's funeral, Neil came by to pick me up. Brent had invited me to go to a club in Detroit where Destroy All Monsters was playing. I had said I didn't think I really could. He said he'd put me on the guest list just in case.

Neil hadn't really wanted to go, though he fiercely refused to let me go alone. He dawdled, and had to go to a camera store in Redford to drop off his projector for repairs, and stop at home to do something, and then go over to Dave's to drink pop and snicker for a couple of hours. So it was nearly eleven-thirty by the time we got to the club.

I wasn't on any guest list; they'd never heard of me. But they let us pay the cover and get in without checking our I.D.s. We came in on the very end of the set. Niagara was just winding up a nice bashy rendition of "You're Gonna Die."

Neil warmed to little, weary, sloe-eyed Niagara in her black corset and leather miniskirt, and warmed to the club itself. He even got up to dance with me after the band took a break. This was amazing, albeit the jukebox was playing Average White Band, but someone soon kicked the thing till that stopped and put on "God Save the Queen" instead. In less than five seconds I had been knocked to the floor. I was utterly enchanted. Everybody started to pounce.

I was pulled to my feet. "Jump, woman!" shouted a bottle-blond young starveling by my side. Within seconds I had learned the Pogo and was snarling along with the crowd, "*Nooo fuuuture!*"

Neil had given up and was back at the bar, looking Godardian, sipping a gin he had managed to acquire despite state regulations. I was suddenly the belle of the ball. All the cadaverous black-clad males wanted me. At last, all that effort with the Cleopatra look finally paid off. I broke away, though, and went towards the restrooms. I thought I saw Brent.

He was there in a dirty pink hallway, wearing an antique tweed jacket and a beret. He was very stoned. He looked at me kindly with moist, many-capillaried eyes, and gave me greeting.

"You made it?" he shouted, over the music. I nodded.

He stood against the wall, nodding. I waited.

He said something. I shrugged, not making it out.

"Funeral's over?" he called out to me, syllable by syllable.

I affirmed it.

"Ahhh," he said.

I waited. He leaned over, said in my ear:

"Come with me to the Green Room."

He took me to the little room, not green, of course, where the entertainers were relaxing, and introduced me to Destroy All Monsters: lanky Larry Miller and his twin brother Ben; Michael Davis, formerly of the MC5, with his warm, gaunt smile of exhausted experience; Ron Asheton, late of the Stooges, burly and friendly; and his ladylove, delicate Niagara, reminding me of one of my cousins. She offered me a Tab.

The band collected itself and went out for its next set. I was becoming aware that it must have appeared that I had abandoned my date, such as he was. But I didn't care, I was mad at him. I stayed and watched Brent stand there for a while, so still and serene. I was sick of him too, him and his guest list.

The band struck up "Assassination Photograph." The music was irresistible; I had to join it. "You're going?" said Brent. He looked like a dog watching ghosts.

"Just—you know—out there," I said.

I was nearly out the door when I was seized from behind. His arms locked around my neck. Mf! I went limp, my heart pounding.

I felt his hair brush the side of my face, his breath against my neck. "'I, a poor peasant, have conquered science,'" he susurrated. "'Why-can't-I-conquer-love!'"

He must have felt me arch and stiffen in delight; he released me then, and I scampered away, looking back for just one second to see the roiling satisfaction on his face. I went out and danced like a mad thing.

8. THANK YOU, MR. MOTO

My mother always used to tell the story of how when I was four years old and wasn't allowed to cross the street by myself, let alone go all the way to the party store for penny candy without adult supervision, I and my friend from across the street, also four, went to my mom and told her that my friend's mother was taking us to the party store. The we went to my friend's mother and told her my mother was taking us, and then my friend and I went to the store by ourselves and got our candy.

I told my mother my father was going to take me up to college, and she was so offended she barely looked at me the last few days I was home. Of course dad assumed mom was taking me.

I took clothes and books and my typewriter. Well, that's about all you have, at that age. Mom stayed in the back of the house while I loaded everything into the hatch of Brent's beetle. Neil and Dave were coming too to help me move, and of course as a rationale to go to Ann Arbor. It was a hot, damp day, and there was no air conditioning, not in my house, not in the car, not in the dorm when we got there.

South Quad was centrally located—you could say that for it. It looked like one of the Brewster projects downtown. By now I was fully aware that I was assigned to what was commonly acknowledged as the least desirable residence hall on campus. (Jennifer and I had stood in line at the housing office to ask for my reassignment to her dorm, but they'd closed before we could get in.) Another thing about South Quad I learned: it was where they'd be putting the football players that year. You'll hear them in the middle of the night, they said, kicking out the glass in the candy machines.

It seemed when we arrived that I would be the first one to move in that day. We didn't see anyone else. But it was a vast building and people had already set up housekeeping here and there, we discovered as we prowled through the wings trying to follow the directions they'd given us at the front desk to find my room. Through open doors, you could hear them already at the windows, screaming "West Quad sucks!" as voices echoed back from the other side of the street, "South Quad sucks!" It was an ongoing rivalry, we were told; it would go on all fall long.

We found my room. It was like the rooms at Marian Hospital, only smaller. There were three dressers, three desks, and three cots. Neither of the other girls were in. But one had already put her bedspread on the cot by the window and her study lamp and pens on the desk nearby, and her clothes filled one of the two closets. The woman at the desk had said overcrowding was going to be a problem that year.

I was early. My classes didn't start for another four days, so I had plenty of time to play. But what was there to do? We had seen all the films in the first-run theaters, and the only film society show that night was *King of Hearts*. "Let's drive to L.A.," said Brent. "We could get there in four days."

But then it would take four days to get back.

"It's up to you," said Brent.

We went to Pizza Bob's so I could get a hot fudge milk shake, and discussed this further. Neil and Dave were actually very excited by the idea. They guessed that you could probably get a cheap motel in Anaheim or in the Valley. But you wouldn't want to stay in L.A. itself, or least of all Hollywood, which was disgusting, Neil said, especially at night. Really, I'd had no idea. I'd thought it was all like Beverly Hills.

It was something to consider. We all hesitated to move my belongings into that dark little box, already occupied by an unseen stranger, and I certainly didn't want to go back to Prague. It was decided that Neil and Dave would take Brent's car and go home and get what they needed for a possible cross-country trip, and stop at Brent's to pick up some things. "Get, like, my Borsalino," said Brent, "and the box of tapes off the top of my bookcase." When they got back, we'd all decide what to do.

There was a certain strain involved in all this. I wanted more than anything to take a nap. But I couldn't do it with Brent in the room with me, and it seemed mean to make him go away while I slept. So instead of going back to South Quad, we went bummeling along State Street.

We came up to his radio station. I asked if he wanted to go in for a while. "Na," he said, "I'm not there anymore."

We went to the comics store at State and William, then round the corner of Liberty to Dave's Books. There, among the SF paperbacks, Brent found a copy of Philip Jose Farmer's *The Image of the Beast*, a Playboy edition with a zaftig raven-haired woman striding across the cover in bikini underwear, a little man-headed snake wound around her lower leg (NOT where he was in the book.) "This is really a find," said Brent. "You should have this. Specially if you're going to L.A."

He bought it for me, and also a Robert Anton Wilson for himself. In sort of a book hunger now, we prowled down to State Street Books, then Border's, and then across the diag to the Grad Library, where he led me off the beaten paths of corridors and stairways into the deep stacks.

You could get very lost in those stacks. They had been built up in sections over decades, and none of the additions logically connected with the others. In the older parts there were little metal stairways poking up through holes cut in the floor, but they only took you to other parts of that section. Not all of the wings of the building connected with one another, so unless you knew where you were going you could get trapped in an egressless section, running ratlike, testing doors by trial and error to see if they'd take you anywhere. There were elevators but they didn't stop on every floor, and sometimes the doors opened in front and sometimes behind you. The stacks went from floor to ceiling and were so close together in places you'd brush the spines of the books on both sides when you turned around. We could hear people around us as we went through the stacks, but we never saw anybody.

"I've always wanted to hide here one night and get locked in. When they'd turn out the light," said Brent, leaning against a shelful

of rare bound 19th century journals and dreamily lighting an absolutely forbidden cigarette. "It'd be pitch black. And then . . . they'd
release the dogs."

When we came back to South Quad, Neil and Dave were already
there, lounging against the broken vending machines. "Well," said
Dave, "what's it going to be, then?"

I looked at Brent. "It's a go, Dr. Go . . . gol," I said.

* * *

When I found out he had been a junkie, I was shocked but not surprised. It fit. Youngkin says he got onto morphine at about the time
he started his theatrical career in earnest, in the late twenties. The
official story is he started taking it as a painkiller during a serious
illness. But what does it matter whether it was a legitimate prescription or something slipped to him backstage by some Weimar Republic
Dr. Feelgood? Show people are subject to kinds of pain we can know
nothing about.

It would explain that mortifyingly out-of-control performance in
Secret Agent. Donald Spoto says as much in *Dark Side of Genius*. It
makes you wonder. That mesmerizing concentration of his: was it the
boy or the drug?

According to Brecht biographer James Lyon, when he was in
New York in early 1947 (around the time those girls Holden Caulfield
tried to pick up saw him buying a newspaper) he got in trouble with
the narcs. Brecht tried to help him during this crisis, not completely
disinterestedly. HUAC was on his tail, and he was laying plans for
scooting over to East Germany and setting up his Berliner Ensemble.
Once he'd gone over the wall, he tried to lure his famous protégé with
a devilishly seductive poem urging him to shed his old existence
and come where he was truly needed. Lyons thinks he didn't join
Brecht because he was afraid the Communist rulers of East Berlin
wouldn't be as tolerant of his addiction as the Americans were (or
at least as easy to pay off). It seems to me it may also have
occurred to him that, having escaped one antisemitic totalitarian

regime with his head unbroken, it wouldn't be so smart to walk right back into another one.

A couple of years later he did go back to Germany, where he did a rather astounding thing. He got together backers and collaborators and wrote, directed, and starred in *Der Verlorene*, the first postwar German-language film to deal with Nazism. It was a weirdly moving gesture towards his former compatriots who had slaughtered six million of his coreligionists, and cruelly used him to justify it. (Some monstrous documentarian had spliced his great *M* speech into an infamous Nazi propaganda film, making it look like a Jew's confession of his own moral degeneracy and need to be exterminated.) His mad, heroic little film was received coldly by the Germans, which apparently devastated him. By making it, he had revealed more of himself than he had intended; it really is the autobiography of a lost soul. It shows how twisted his perceptions of himself and his own possibilities had become that, given this opportunity to throw off that hated typecasting and invent the perfect showcase for himself, he chose to play a homicidal Nazi mad doctor.

Meanwhile, on the other side of the barbed wire, Brecht dangled great roles at him. He even offered him Hamlet. Though he may not have let him hear his snide aside that it wasn't bad casting, as Shakespeare offers clues that Hamlet was fat.

You could tell he was bored in his later films. The lack of energy, the reliance on mechanical bits of business: the gesture he first used in *M*, the clawed fingers drawn down the face, pulling the feature into fleeting monstrous distortion (viz. *The Beast with Five Fingers*). Or the trick of making a little smile that suddenly melts into something quite unlike a smile, a la *Secret Agent*. As age and creeping ugliness overtook him, the occult virility inherent in his early performances softened; just the effort of trying to talk, of padding around in that puffy, druggy old body seemed excruciating.

The Patsy. The Buster Keaton Story. It could have been different. Brecht thought he was fit for stage work in the fifties, and maybe he was; why not? The Theatre of the Absurd was made for him. Think of him waiting for Godot, or thundering around turning into a rhinoceros. If he'd lived a few years longer, in better health, couldn't you see him, grizzled and crackling with wit as the old Marquis de Sade discoursing on man's inhumanity to man with Marat in his bath? And what about film? Wouldn't Herzog or Fassbinder have come up with something amazing for him, if he'd lasted that long? But. The claws of the sea puss get us all in the end.

*   *   *

"Now that we've violated the Mann Act," said Brent, lighting a doob as we crossed the Ohio border.

The lady at AAA had mapped out a route for us in orange marker. It was the old 66 route. The worst roller coaster ride on this earth, ratcheting up to Chicago, with a sickening drop through the flatlands, catching it in the rear at the base of Missouri, then bouncing through the Southwest over what the Trip-Tik euphemistically terms "softly rolling hills." The worst at first seems to be coming down from Flagstaff through the Coconino forest, approaching what looks like a near-sheer drop off a mountain. Surviving that through some inscrutable force of gravity, you enter the Living Desert, Krazy Kat country, those familiar bleak sand flats and porcupine brush clumps. Then, as in *Lawrence of Arabia*, you have to traverse the Anvil of the Sun, the Mojave. We did it in the dead of night to keep our tires from melting.

"Look at this," said Dave, "how black it is. The headlights are the only lights. Look." And he turned them off to demonstrate. We screamed them back on again.

The sun came up just in time for us to find our way up to that revolting vertical mountain entrance to San Bernardino that says to you every inch you go up it, "Are you sure you really want to go to L.A.?" I kept my eyes shut till I felt the beetle go level again, and heard Dave and Brent screaming, "And CU-CA-MONGAAA!!!"

When we got to Glendale it was 7 A.M., and we were a day ahead of schedule. My three drivers had been too keyed up on ambition and No-Doz (or what Brent *said* was No-Doz) to stop. Brent had chosen our resting place well. It was a sweet little stone-and-orange-wrought-iron motor court off the main stem, near lots of movie theaters, notably the Alex, where the studios used to preview things when they wanted a test audience of people like us.

We all went in to the front desk; none of us wanted to stay in that beetle a moment longer. There was a little man behind the desk with thick plastic glasses, and there was a gust of sandalwood scent that nearly knocked you over. Whether it came from the man or room, I couldn't tell.

We asked for a single, as usual, and for once were not stared at. I got into the bed, and as our custom went they spread out on the floor in their sleeping bags. I was nearly prostrate; we'd barely slept since we left Ann Arbor, but the moment I closed my eyes they turned on the television and found a movie. It was *The Garden of Allah*, the one about the defrocked monk who gets together with Marlene Dietrich in a tent. "Oh my glory, it's Charles Boyer," said Brent.

"Look at that itto face," said Dave. "Sort of like P.L.'s normal brother. Did they make any movies together?"

I recollected *Confidential Agent* and *The Constant Nymph*.

"And *Around the World in 80 Days*," said Neil.

"She likes him, don't you. He's everything you want in a man. Short, dark, dead, and in black and white."

"He's dead?"

"Last month. His wife died, he didn't want to be alone so he took some pills."

"Aw. That's really romantic. I mean, what a nice guy."

"Hey you dead ladee, come with me to the Casbah."

"He never said that, he was already in the Casbah, that was the whole point! He couldn't come out or the cops would get him."

"P.L. was in that one wasn't he?"

"No, that was Joseph Calleia. He was in the remake, the musical. *Casbah*."

"Man, I *love* a good Peter Lorre musical."

"Look. Here's my Charles Boyer impression."

Dave suddenly posed in cruelly accurate mockery of Boyer's anguished expression in the sustained close-up that seemed to have been

2326-SHAR

on the TV screen for ten minutes now: lips outsplayed from clenched teeth, eyelids spread in a slightly goofy expression of alarmed passion. "Now who's this." The demented finger-drag down the face, a la *Beast with Five Fingers*. Then, lips pooched out and twisted, head twitching, hands gnarling together: "*Therredschooz!*"

"Amazing," said Neil.

And poor Charles Boyer, still up on that screen, insensate to all in his guilt-crazed desperation, stammered out the secrets of his tormented psyche. I struggled to catch what he was saying so urgently. A man had told him something, something that had seemed to him—unclean. Then later, looking out the window of his solitary monastery cell, he saw that unclean man kiss a woman—they seemed to him to have the faces of— angels! Then later, gazing out that window at the city over the monastery walls, he thought: they are living there, those people!

"Are we bugging you?" asked Brent, intruding his big face in front of Charles Boyer's.

He leaned down close. "Come with me," he said.

* * *

They say Middle Americans always feel at home in Los Angeles because they've seen so much of it on television. But my sense of recognition was something even eerier. Had this whole trip been just an illusion of travel, and had I stepped instead into a counter-earth version of the place I'd thought I'd left?

Hollywood looked to me like Royal Oak: Hollywood Boulevard was Main Street, Sunset Boulevard was Woodward Avenue, and the Chinese Theatre was Father Coughlin's Shrine of the Little Flower. Downtown L.A. was Detroit, with its foul gray abandoned blocks crawling with scary bent-over people. Anaheim was Prague, with its freeway exits and strip malls, and Disneyland instead of the Church Block.

Brent drove me down Los Feliz, past the train station Barbara Stanwyck used in *Double Indemnity*, across the street from Forest Lawn, the original of *The Loved One*. Bogart was buried there, but Bogart's little friend wasn't, possibly because they didn't take Jews. I didn't want to go in. We drove on into the barrio, round MacArthur Park where the green cake melted, past the locations of several Laurel and Hardy shorts and into Hollywood proper.

With that serene confidence I now realized was either hard-wired into his brain or chemically induced on a sempiternal basis, he negotiated down Santa Monica Boulevard, past studios and wig shops to Hollywood Memorial Cemetery. He parked. "Now you have to go in," he said.

"We're not dressed to go in there!"

"Doesn't matter. They're used to tourists."

Me in my shorts and zorries and Brent in his Mothership Connection T-shirt. At least I could bring him a tribute, to show respect. There was a little florist's outside the entrance that gouged you for this purpose. I fretted over what was proper. Roses were morbid, and lilies were unspeakable, and anyway everything was too feminine. I finally picked a single carnation of a sort of peach color. Luckily it was a weekday and we seemed to be the only ones there, so no one would know who left it.

Brent had a book of Neil's that had a map of all the crypts. We found him right away, at the end of a long corridor lined with Armenians. There was nothing to mark him as anyone famous. There was a little brass plaque with his name and dates and those of his last wife, the one he'd had a child with, and who'd been about to divorce him when he died. There was a little vase there where I could put the stupid carnation, after breaking off its too-long stem. Brent was standing by, hands folded, actually not smiling. He was Catholic, and knew what to do.

And I realized with a little panic that I didn't. What do you do at a gravesite, pray? I couldn't use the Catholic prayers I'd learned because I didn't believe in them. What else was there, the Kaddish? I didn't know it, and it seemed to me women weren't supposed to say it anyway. I remembered something about paying someone to say it for you, but even if there was someone available for this should I even presume? My own religion didn't provide you with anything you could bring to such a place. All I could think was that here was a person who'd lived in this city, and done his work here, and bought this little nook (which must have been prime property—of course, the neighborhood had come down since then). And now he was dead, just as I'd be someday.

Early in his Hollywood career, publicists had put around stories that he was a "student of psychology," that this was what gave his portrayals of aberrant personalities their compelling power. He actually was known as something of an amateur therapist among his friends; troubled people often do have a talent that way. When Bogart was hesitating to marry Lauren Bacall, worried she was too young for him, he helped talk him into it; he had taken a blonde trophy wife to himself at the time. He told Bogart, go ahead, what if you only have a couple of years together—at least you'll have had those years.

And if he'd seen me at that moment, he'd have said to me: What are you doing hanging around an old man's tomb? You've been watching too many of my movies! Your eyes are all red; go back to bed. Go back to school.

I felt silly, morbid, humiliated, and I was so tired. I started to cry. Brent misunderstood, thought I was cute, and penetrated me with a long and very involved kiss. Then I was too astonished to think of anything else.

He took me down the hall to Valentino, a much more impressive crypt. I said I wondered if the Dark Lady was showing up today. "Hm," said Brent, and seized me and did it again.

People were coming, so he marched me outside among the headstones. But this was no private place. Early as it was, people were roaming in. How carelessly dressed they were, considering who they were coming to see: these people who'd been so concerned about how they appeared to us, their public, when they were alive.

He took me down the street to a coffee shop, where he fed me pancakes from his own fork, gazing and gazing at me. He gave me a puff from his cigarette.

"You won't ever leave me, will you?" he asked.

We walked back towards the car. We hit Hollywood Boulevard as they were hosing down the pavement; they had recently started installing the star-scattered brass plaques with entertainers' names on them and seemed very proud and cautious about them. Turning the corner of the Egyptian to meet us were Neil and Dave. "This is a small town!" said Brent. "How'd you get here?"

"We took the bus in front of the Alex," said Dave.

I tried to fall in step with Neil, but he gently herded me back to my former position, in front with Brent. In a way I couldn't sense yet, but they could. I had been marked out. Dave and Neil and I were still as close as we ever had been, but it was a more ceremonial friendship from this time on. They were wincing in the direct sunlight and didn't look me in the face.

"Maybe I should stay out here," Brent was saying. "We could rent a house and all live together. I could get a radio show. Hmm, they probably don't have punk out here yet."

A couple of living Barbie dolls boomed past us on roller skates, nearly knocking Neil over.

"You can write them and get them to refund your check for the dorm room," Brent was saying. "You can't go back there. The thought of you shut up in that box like an abused veal."

We were in front of Frederick's now. In the window there was a thing in pink and black, very Frankenfurter, that I admired. Brent liked it too.

"If I don't go back," I said, "I'll lose my grant. My mom and dad—"

"It's copacetic," said Brent. "You don't need money here. You hang out till you establish residency, then you can go to UCLA. In-state tuition's practically nothing."

"Really?"

"Sure," said Brent, as though he really was.

"But that could take a whole year. Or more than that!"

"You might be right."

"But what'll I do till then? How will I live?"

Tenderly he put his hand on my neck. "Don't worry," he said. "We'll tell you."

THE END